RECKLESS HEART

The Harts of Texas: Book Three

BARBARA MCMAHON

Reckless Heart
Copyright © 2016 Barbara McMahon
All Rights Reserved

One

Molly Forrester tried not to fidget under the disapproving gaze of the employment agency owner, but it became more difficult when the older woman's face frowned so menacingly. Sarah Montgomery, owner, representative and chief factotum of the Montgomery Employment Agency, reviewed the file before her. Her iron gray hair drawn into a no-nonsense style suited her brusque personality. She dropped her gaze to the thin folder she had opened and scanned her notes.

"This is the third place that has fired you for daydreaming," she said severely.

Molly swallowed hard and tried to think up a convincing answer that would get her one more chance. She needed a job. Clearing her throat, she smiled and nodded. "I admit I was... distracted, but only that one time."

Mrs. Montgomery raised an eyebrow and flicked a glance at the younger woman. "It says you mixed up the orders repeatedly and your milkshakes were more milk than anything."

"I don't think a fast-food restaurant is exactly my

kind of place," Molly said with dignity.

"Miss Forrester, I'm beginning to wonder if anything is your kind of place. We placed you with Bennett, Strife and Harwell as a receptionist."

She referred to the pages that sat on the left of the folder. "You mixed up the telephone messages, hung up on an important client, and were found daydreaming when the phones were ringing off the wall."

Molly nodded, trying to look repentant. She'd found the position tedious and boring.

"When they fired you, we tried Markham's department store. You mixed up the sales register so badly I think they're still trying to straighten it out. You sent merchandise to the wrong address, and you ignored valued customers because you were daydreaming."

Molly dropped her gaze. She didn't need Mrs. Montgomery reciting the past. She knew her mind hadn't been on any of the jobs she'd held.

She wanted to write.

But until she could make a living from writing, she needed a way to earn money to live on.

Growing up the daughter of Gerald Forrester, she had not expected to actually work beyond what she wanted to do—in this case write. Even her brief engagement to Mark Leggett had continued the idea she would be able to forge a career for herself writing books.

That expectation had shattered when she had discovered her father's interference in her engagement. Though it wasn't entirely his fault. Marc had been promised a sure-fire track to the top in her father's business once he was married to Molly.

She hadn't believed he was serious when she first found out. But when she confronted Marc he had easily confessed, thinking it no big deal. Even offering her a lot of freedom in their relationship—a hint of her going her way and he his with their marriage only a business arrangement.

She'd been devastated when she finally accepted the truth of the situation. Confronting her father hadn't helped. He considered it a dynastic alliance. Like they were in mid-evil England or something.

She'd refused to cooperate, returning Marc's ring, and letting her father know she was not going to be used as a pawn for his business ends.

He'd calmly told her not to expect any further financial support until she came to her senses. The first time she'd tried her credit card and been refused she'd known her father wasn't bluffing.

Being the spoiled rich girl of a wealthy man, she'd not been trained for anything, except perhaps being the finest hostess in the state.

She'd moved out and stayed with her friend Bethany, trying to get a job to prove to herself, and to her father, she didn't need to fall in with his wishes just to keep a roof over her head.

"This was the third job in two months," Mrs. Montgomery reiterated.

Molly nodded. A touch of panic shot up her spine. If she didn't get something else right away she'd be out of money.

Bethany was already hinting she'd overstayed her welcome. The last thing she wanted to do was return home and admit her father had been right.

"Can you cook?" Mrs. Montgomery asked.

Molly looked up. "Yes." She wasn't great by any means, but she could prepare simple meals. She'd loved hanging out in the kitchen and learning how to make basic dishes when she'd been a teenager.

"I have a possible position." For once Mrs. Montgomery permitted herself a small smile. "It might be a match made in heaven," she murmured to herself. "Or the fastest dismissal in the agency's records."

"For a cook?" Molly asked.

"For a cook and housekeeper on a ranch outside town."

"I'll take it!"

Mrs. Montgomery obviously disapproved of her enthusiasm. She fixed her disapproving gaze once more on Molly and shook her head slowly. "It's the last thing I have for you, but it won't be easy. Josh Hart's impossible to work for."

"I'm sure I can manage." Molly Forrester smoothed her palms over the plain blue skirt she'd worn for the interview. With the starched white blouse and red blazer, she hoped she looked the epitome of competency. She'd fussed with her curly light brown hair that morning, taming it into a semblance of order. Her makeup was discreet. She needed this job.

"He's had five housekeepers in the last seven months. Four weeks was the longest anyone stayed." Sarah Montgomery's dour comments were no doubt intended to dissuade Molly from pursuing the position. It had no effect.

"I'm sure I can manage." Molly refused to dwell on the possibility that the agency would not send her. Her credentials were scarce, she had very little work experience, and what she had wasn't outstanding by any means. But she could make this assignment work. One way or another she planned to live life on her terms, not her father's.

She'd succeed if the agency would give her the chance.

The older woman peered at Molly over the frames of her half-glasses. If Mrs. Montgomery's intent was to intimidate, Molly thought, she came close to succeeding. But Molly refused to let the older woman know it.

Showing a calm confidence she was far from feeling, Molly returned her gaze. Anticipation simmered in her veins. She had to get the job. And she'd do it to the best of her ability.

"The ranch is over an hour's drive from here."

Molly nodded. That'd suit her fine. She had no need to dash into town. A glimmer of excitement bubbled up inside her. Another chance. One she'd make sure she made work.

"From the reports of the housekeepers who worked there, Josh Hart is bossy, arrogant, and quite demanding. Nothing pleases him."

Molly took a deep breath. He sounded like her father, and Marc. She'd had years of experience dealing with men like that.

Would taking this job be exchanging one tyrant for another?

"I've had experience dealing with similar situations,"

she said calmly.

She knew office work didn't suit her. Nor retail sales. Nor fast-food restaurants. Growing panicked, she crossed her fingers. She wanted this job.

The older woman studied her briefly, dropped her gaze back to the opened folder.

"Very well. I'll call and let him know you are recommended by us. He'll have the final say, of course."

Reaching beside her, she handed a thick envelope to Molly. "Directions to the Rafter C and the terms and conditions of employment. If you have any questions, call me. Good luck, Miss Forrester. You'll need it."

Two

Molly slowed her car to a stop near the large white ranch house. She'd been on Rafter C land for several minutes; the drive from the road to the house had been about a mile in length. On either side cattle grazed on open fields. She saw the house before she reached it situated as it was on a small knoll. The two-story white clapboard farmhouse had a porch on three sides, and dark green shutters on the upper story windows. Grass surrounded the house and a large elm tree shaded the left side.

She drove around to the back of the house, per the directions given in the packet Mrs. Montgomery had given her. The porch that wrapped around three sides of the house stopped short of the back. Instead, there was a small wooden stoop at the top of three steps and a single door.

About a hundred yards from the house sat a huge barn, the gray paint surprising. Weren't all barns painted red? The spanking-white trim sparkled in the mid-morning sun.

She arrived in plenty of time to get settled before preparing lunch. Anxious to prove to her new boss that she was capable of the job, she'd done her best to be prompt and dressed to blend in.

She opened the car door and stepped out, a bit self-conscious. Her jeans were worn and comfortable, as was her cotton T-shirt. Only the boots were new. She didn't have a hat. Not that she planned to spend much time outside—her work was in the house. But a cowboy hat would have been the perfect touch.

Glancing around, Molly noticed several men in and around the barn. One worked with a horse in the large corral, another sat on a turned-up barrel, a tangle of leather straps in his hand that he seemed to be working on.

Two others paused in their tasks as they stopped to watch her. A tall man came from inside the barn at the sound of her car. She shielded her eyes against the sun's glare with the palm of her hand and waited. Her heart thumped in her chest as she watched him approach.

She didn't believe in time travel, but suddenly wondered if she were wrong. He looked like a Viking. Tall, several inches over six feet, broad, blond. He strode across the dusty yard as if a conqueror returning home. His stride swiftly ate up the distance. He slapped his hat against his thigh, dislodging a speck of hay while the sun's rays burnished the thick blond hair like old Spanish doubloons. His eyes narrowed as he studied her, drawing closer every second.

Molly took a deep breath and dropped her hand, her eyes fixed on him.

Slowly a smile lit her face. Hero material was scarce. Yet right before her eyes stood the perfect specimen.

Greedily her gaze traveled from his broad shoulders across his muscular chest to his slim waist, hips, muscular thighs. The jeans displayed his masculine attributes to perfection. The dusty boots completed the image.

She raised her eyes, anxious for a pen and paper to capture the sensations that jostled around inside, to capture for all time the decidedly feminine feelings that flooded her being, the unexpected delight she discovered in merely watching him.

When her gaze reached his face, his scowling expression jolted her back to awareness of where she was and why she was here.

"Lost?" he asked, setting the hat on his head, tilted down to shadow his eyes.

She shook her head and smiled again. The spiraling sense of anticipation that tantalized her shimmered unexpectedly. The urge to step closer, feel his heat, align herself with him, was totally foreign. Yet she found herself hard-pressed to resist.

"I'm Molly Forrester, your new housekeeper."

His look became incredulous as he trailed his gaze down her slim figure, pausing briefly at the shiny new boots. He shook his head as his eyes drifted back to hers.

"Is this some kind of joke?" he asked.

"No." Reaching into the car, she withdrew the employment packet and pulled Mrs. Montgomery's letter from the stack. "Mrs. Montgomery said she'd be calling you. Didn't you talk with her yet?"

Josh Hart took the letter, scanned it briefly then looked at Molly.

Mrs. Montgomery had called yesterday to inform him she'd found him yet another housekeeper, a Molly Forrester. But she'd neglected to mention the woman was young and pretty and totally unsuitable for the job.

For heaven's sake, he could smell roses from where he stood.

His gaze traveled over her again. She had to be years younger than he. And far too feminine. She curved in all the right places, not that he cared. He'd sworn off women himself, but he didn't need the distraction she'd cause the men.

She didn't look capable of staying the course. Probably some fluffy-headed woman who thought living on a ranch was all fun and games. Or planned to flirt with the men disrupting everything.

Or was she looking to hook a rancher, like Jeannie?

What had the agency been thinking? Just because he'd had five housekeepers since Rachel left was no excuse to send this one. None of the others had been worth a damn. Yet each one of them offered more than this little slip of a woman could.

"Sorry you had the drive out, you won't do." He folded the letter and handed it back to Molly.

Molly blinked in shock. "What do you mean, I won't do? You haven't interviewed me, haven't had me cook anything. Besides, as I heard it, you don't have much choice. I'm the best you've got right now."

She wouldn't let this one opportunity amount to nothing. She slammed the car door and stepped closer to the man.

"Are you Josh Hart?" she asked, making sure she

was talking to the boss, not some foreman or flunky who thought he'd throw his weight around.

"Right. Boss of the Rafter C. Around here what I say goes and I say you won't do," he replied.

Molly glanced around for support.

While the cowboys watched them, they'd resumed their work. No one was going to help from there.

Turning back to face him, she stepped closer, her fists on her hips, she wanted to scream, but settled for asking through clenched teeth,

"And where are all the other housekeepers who are so much better than I? As I see it, Mr. Hart, you don't have anyone else."

She knew this. He knew this.

"Maybe you should consider giving me a try before throwing me off your ranch." She'd already packed her things and thanked Bethany for putting up with her. She had nowhere else to go and no other job prospects. She'd make this one work. She would make sure of it. The last thing in the world she wanted was to return home to her father in defeat.

He reached out and took one of her fists, prying open the fingers and smoothing his thumb across the soft skin of her palm. Molly was perplexed by his totally unexpected touch.

"Working on a ranch is hard work. Your hands are too soft to have done anything even close to what's required here," Josh said, his thumb moving back and forth.

Molly tried to pull away but his grip held firm. She glared at him. "I'm not here to do ranch work. I'm here to do housework. How hard do you think that is?"

"Harder than you're used to," he retorted.

She held his gaze with effort.

He hit close to home but she refused to acknowledge it. She suddenly found it difficult to think with her hand firmly held by his. She drew in a deep breath—tried to rein her clamoring senses under some control.

"Who does the work now?" she asked.

Josh shrugged, his thumb still rubbing across her palm. His eyes dropped to the movement, as if mesmerized by the soft feel of her skin.

He didn't know this woman's history, but he'd bet she never worked a day in her life.

Taking a deep breath, the gentle scent of roses that surrounded them filled his nostrils. "The men and I are making do until the next housekeeper arrives."

"Then your troubles are over. I've arrived."

He shook his head.

"Normally—" She cleared her throat. What was normal about a man holding her hand? Nothing. Her heart pounded. Her skin tingled at his touch. Tugging, she freed herself and involuntarily stepped back. The glare in his steely gray eyes unnerved her. Yet she needed this job more than anything. It was her last chance. She refused to meekly climb back into her car and head back to her father's home.

"Normally what?" he asked.

"Normally, do the men cook?"

"The ranch had a housekeeper that had been here for years. When her mother became ill and needed her, she left. Normal changed when she left. One of these days the agency will send someone appropriate who will stay as long as Rachel did and the problem will go away."

Molly smiled, hoping the fear of not getting the job didn't show. "It looks to me as if you don't have much choice. According to the agency, you've driven the others away. The Montgomery Agency couldn't get anyone else, so you're stuck with me."

He frowned, as if he disliked hearing the situation put into words. "Or I can go to another agency."

"With the same results is my guess. Five housekeepers in seven months isn't a great track record it seems to me." Where were the words coming from? She'd rarely stood up to her father, how could she stand up to this giant of a man?

"And you'll do better? The longest any of them stayed was four weeks."

Molly nodded. "I'll stay longer than four weeks. And be the best housekeeper you've ever had."

She kept the smile plastered on her face, hoping he couldn't see how her heart raced.

Josh didn't want her to stay. Here only ten minutes and she reminded him of his ex-fiancée, Jeannie. Not in looks. Jeannie had been tall and blonde. This woman stood shorter, barely up to his chin, with light brown hair that waved as soft as silk around her face.

For a split second temptation swept through him to brush his fingers through the waves to see if they were as soft as they looked. Clenching his hands into fists, he resisted the urge. A pretty face had misled him before. He wouldn't go that route again.

She was too young, too much temptation to keep around.

He wanted a woman of fifty or older with grown kids and a lifetime of keeping house. A woman like he remembered his mother, who'd relished ranch life, enjoyed cooking for the men and sharing in the conversation at dinner that centered on cattle, market price of beef, and rodeos. Not some flighty young thing that looked as if a puff of strong Texas wind would blow her away.

Yet she had a point. His house was a disaster. He hunted for clean clothes every day—hated doing laundry.

His men were grumbling with the catch-as-catch-can cooking. One had quit last month, refusing to take another turn cooking. Even Lance, his foreman, had grumbled and threatened to look for another job if he had to cook another meal.

And not one of the over-fifty housekeepers that had come to work had stayed.

He was going to say yes. And live to regret it—he knew it.

Yet she clearly stated the situation—he desperately needed someone. For however long she stayed, he could use the help.

In the meantime, he'd call the agency and tell them to continue looking.

"We'll give it a try. My guess is you won't last a week," he conceded.

Molly nodded and looked away, trying to hide her delight. If she could do the job, she'd do just fine until she finished her book. Living on the premises would allow her to save almost all her salary.

If the book sold, then she could decide whether to stay until it became published or move to an apartment to write another one.

There was plenty of time to decide that in the future. She'd barely arrived.

Ideas crowded her thoughts. A dozen more sprang to mind from seeing Josh Hart. With her own fertile imagination, and the quiet setting of the ranch in which to create, she should have the book she'd already started completed within a few weeks, a couple of months at the most. Then there'd be no stopping her.

"Come on, I'll show you around the place. You can unpack and get lunch ready before starting anything else. There are seventeen ranch hands plus you and me. Can you cook for a crowd that size?"

"Sure."

How hard could it be? She'd just multiply what she wanted to eat by 20. She knew from the cook at home that men like lots of hearty meals. Nothing frou-frou or fancy would be the rule.

"We eat at six, one and seven. Sometimes later if we're branding or dipping."

She nodded, wondering what branding and dipping were. Then wondering why he'd had such a hard time getting anyone to stay. Three meals a day, even if one was at six in the morning, a quick flick of the dust cloth and the rest of the day would be hers. Of course, one or two days a week she'd have to vacuum and do laundry according to the list of duties she'd read. Aside from that, there should be plenty of time available to write.

She smiled. She was here and she wasn't budging.

Josh's long stride quickly covered the distance between her car and the stoop at the back door. His boots rang loud on the wood as he skipped the second step and hit the third. Molly hurried to keep up. She'd show him—

Oops. Her slick boot sole slipped off the edge of the step. Flinging her arms out to try to avoid a fall, she encircled Josh's thigh, slamming against him with her full weight. He lurched, unable to catch his balance because of her death grip, tumbling off the narrow porch with a loud thump. Molly followed him down, crashing against him as they both landed in the dirt.

"Oh, no. I'm so sorry." Scrambling, Molly knelt on the dirt, her hand on his thigh.

"Oh, Mr. Hart, are you all right? I'm so sorry."

Ineffectively she patted his leg, wondering if she'd killed her new boss.

When he raised up on one elbow and glared at her, she knew she hadn't. Though maybe it might have been better for her if she had. Anger shone in his eyes. His body seemed to grow in stature.

"There are several steps there," he said through gritted teeth. "You are to take them one at a time."

"I know. I...my boot slipped."

He sat up and looked at her kneeling on the dirt. "Trouble walking?" he growled sarcastically.

"It was an accident. Surely even the boss of the Rafter C has had an accident on occasion."

He rose, reached down to grasp her upper arm and hauled her to her feet. Waiting until she had her balance before releasing her, he muttered something under his breath.

"What?"

"Nothing." He took a deep breath. "Accidents do happen. Come on."

Holding open the door, he ushered her into the large country kitchen. It looked as if a wall had been knocked out between the kitchen and what had been the dining room. A long trestle table took up most of the room. Quickly she noted there were twenty chairs around it. She expected they'd all be filled at dinner, or all but a couple. The reality was starting to sink in. She hoped she could feed that many at one time.

But before then there was a lot of work to do. The kitchen was a mess. Dishes soaked in cold water, a thin film of congealed grease floating on top. Dirt gritted beneath her feet as she walked into the room. The windows were bare of curtains, the table needed wiping.

"Looks like I got here just in time," she said, hiding her dismay.

"I never said I didn't need anyone. Just that you won't do."

What was the man's problem? His disapproval was odd—he didn't know her from a hole in the wall. Why did he think she couldn't handle the job?

Tilting her chin, Molly silently vowed she'd prove to be the best housekeeper he ever had.

And when she sold her book and was ready to move on, he'd beg her to stay. He'd grovel at her feet for ever doubting her. And she'd turn up her nose and walk away without a backward glance.

She'd show him!

"Pantry and freezer are through there." He pointed to a door on the side wall. "Might need to get some things. We've been too busy working outside to mess much with shopping and such."

"That's what I'm here for. Why don't you go on back outside and do what you were doing and I'll get things settled in here."

Molly didn't want him hanging around while she tried to bring some order out of this chaos. She knew she wasn't superwoman, but anyone with a lick of sense could at least clean up a bunch of dirty dishes.

Then she'd see to lunch.

"Molly Forrester."

She swung around. "What?"

"Just verifying that's your name." He studied her with his silvery eyes seeming to see down into her soul.

For a heartbeat, she felt a tug of attraction. Which she immediately clamped down on. She wanted no distractions in any form. She had come to escape a domineering father who thought he had the right to run her life for her. And a faux fiancé who had followed her father's lead.

She wanted to establish herself in a career of her choosing. She wasn't going to get sidetracked from her goal. The last thing she wanted was to feel any attraction toward her new boss. Or any other cowboy on the ranch.

Not that she could totally ignore Josh Hart, of course. He was the perfect example of what a man should look like in her mind. She'd have to be dead to deny that. Not that she'd let herself act upon any attraction at all. She knew all about men. How they wanted women to wait on them hand and foot. How they derided any attempts to grow and develop. How they ignored her needs and wanted to use her for their own ends.

She'd escaped that life. She'd observe the cowboys on the ranch and use them in her book. She'd research what they liked and what they didn't. And it'd be strictly research, no personal involvement. She'd keep herself aloof and dedicated to doing the best job she could.

She wasn't staying for life. Once her book sold, she'd move on.

"You all right?" Josh asked, shaking her arm a little.

Blinking, Molly nodded. She'd been daydreaming again. She had to watch that, it caused more trouble than she wanted in the past. She dare not let it affect this job.

"A bit daunted by the task ahead, but I can manage."

He was too observant to let her slip away in her mind like she did so often and let it go unnoticed.

She didn't need that escape anymore. She'd left her father's house and life and had no intentions of ever returning.

He glanced around. "Wouldn't take Rachel long to clean this up."

"My guess is Rachel would never have let it get this bad," she replied tartly. "Don't you have work to do?"

"Miss Forrester, in case you were wondering, I run this spread, not you."

"I'm just trying to ease you out the door so I can get to work. I don't need supervision to wash dishes."

She turned to face him. Big mistake. He stood too

close. For the first time in ages, Molly wondered what she looked like. Had her lipstick worn off? Had the breeze in the yard tangled her hair? Did her clothes fit all right?

Swallowing hard, she wished she dare move. Either a step back for safety's sake, or a step forward so she could feel his heat, breathe in the scent of him that she'd caught when they had tangled on the stoop.

"There will be five of us in for lunch. The rest of the men won't be back until supper. Can you manage?"

"Yes."

She watched him shake his head in doubt and head back outside.

Josh paused on the stoop and gazed at the men near the barn. He'd tell them they had a housekeeper, but not to grow too used to the idea. He couldn't imagine this hothouse flower managing a single day, much less for the foreseeable future.

He'd give her the chance, though. As she'd said, he didn't have any options. His sister had told him he needed someone the last time she'd been here. Not that he needed telling. Trying to do things around the house when there was so much to do around the ranch was impossible. He wouldn't call on his older brother for help, either. Jase had given years of his life to building the ranch to the spread it was now.

The least Josh could do is keep it going strong.

He set his hat on his head and started for the barn, wondering how long Molly Forrester would last.

Breathing a sigh of relief when Josh Hart left the kitchen, Molly turned to the mess awaiting her. It didn't look as if she would be writing anything today. Once she cleaned up the kitchen, she'd need to fix lunch for the cowboys. And then plan a meal for dinner.

Sometime during the afternoon, she'd unpack, and get her laptop set up. At least she could do that much today.

She wanted to explore the house, see which room would likely be hers. But first, she had to get this kitchen in better shape than now.

By the time the men streamed in for lunch, Molly managed to clean all the dishes, wipe down the counters, table and stove and sweep the floor.

She'd rummaged around in the cupboards and pantry and begun a list of food items to purchase to feed the crew at Rafter C. The supplies available were limited. It was long past time someone went shopping.

She'd done her best with lunch—but it was a pitiful array that met the eyes of the hungry cowboys.

Peanut butter and jelly sandwiches mingled with grilled cheese on two large platters in the center of the table. There were small bowls of canned soup at each place: vegetable, beef barley and cream of mushroom. A huge pot of black coffee kept warm on the stove. At least there was plenty of that.

Josh walked to the head of the table and stared at the platters. Slowly he raised his gaze to hers. His disbelief was blatant. "This is lunch?"

She nodded, suddenly wary. There was little food to be had. She'd done her best. Seeing his frown of disapproval, she instantly knew it wasn't enough.

The other men sank down in the chairs, silent as

they surveyed the stacks of sandwiches, the bowls of mismatched soup. As one, they all looked at Molly.

She smiled brightly. "I'm Molly Forrester."

No one said a word.

"The new housekeeper."

"Where did you work before, ma'am, at a nursery school?" one of the older men asked.

"Get started. I'll be back in a minute," Josh said.

Gripping Molly's arm, he marched her from the room and down the hall to the room he used as his office. Slamming the door behind him, he spun her around until they faced each other.

"Is lunch supposed to be a joke?" he asked. "Or is this your idea of being what I needed for a housekeeper? These are hardworking, hungry men. Not some ladies at a tea!"

Molly felt like a failure. There had been limited supplies granted—however if she'd been a true housekeeper, she'd have known how to fix something else for hardworking men.

Peanut butter and jelly suddenly seemed childish and not very filling. But once she had finished washing all the dirty dishes, there hadn't been much time to prepare a full-blown meal, not with food readily available.

The heat of his anger washed through her. Blinking in surprise, she stood her ground, a matching anger beginning to build.

"It's no joke. It's all I found to feed this crew. If you want to eat better you should buy more food!"

"So do we expect a kid's happy meal for dinner?"

She ignored his scathing tone and shook her head.

"I have time to go into town and get some food for dinner."

"All the men will be in for dinner, that's seventeen plus you and me. You told me you could manage to feed that many. Having second thoughts?"

Josh had been mad clear through when he first saw the skimpy platter of sandwiches. Yet she looked so determined meeting his gaze with anger in her own eyes, he had a hard time holding on to his anger. He was not getting soft with some stranger, no matter how pretty!

"These men engage in hard physical labor all day long. We need a lot of food to keep going. And we prefer something with a bit more substance than peanut butter."

"It was in the cupboard, I assumed it was to be used," she snapped back. She knew she'd blown it. But there had not been a big selection. At least everyone had food to eat.

"Probably for Rachel or one of the other housekeepers. I don't remember being served peanut butter and jelly sandwiches since my mother died."

She stood tall and nodded, tilting her chin.

"I stand corrected. In the future I'll make sure there are ham and cheese and roast beef sandwiches."

She gritted her teeth lest the words tumbling around her mind spilled out. So she had a bit to learn. It would help if there were some food around to prepare. She'd stock up the kitchen with so much food there'd always be choices for the lots and lots of meals.

"The grilled cheese sandwiches were a good idea. I hope there are one or two left when we get back in there," he conceded.

"If there'd been more cheese or bread, I would have fixed more. Your pantry is practically bare, your refrigerator has more green stuff growing in it than your yard, and the freezer holds sides of cows, not nice little packets that could be quickly thawed and used."

"If you can't do the job—"

She whirled around and stormed across the office in anger.

Was that his out, fire her after one meal? She wasn't going to give in easily over this. She needed this job. And he needed a housekeeper.

She turned to face him before leaving the room, feeling braver with the distance between them.

"I arrived here a couple of hours ago. I needed to shovel out the dirt you accumulated in that kitchen over the last who knows how long, then scrounge around for food to feed over half a dozen people. I'm a writer, not a magician. I can't clean off enough plates to eat from and conjure up food all with a wave of my hand. I did fine for what raw materials I had to work with. Once I get some shopping done, everything will be fine!"

"A writer?" Josh repeated, picking up on the word. "You're a writer?"

She closed her eyes briefly. Stupid! She hadn't wanted anyone to know until she sold a book. Not after the mocking comments of her father and Marc.

"I thought you were a housekeeper. You're a writer?" Josh asked suspiciously.

She opened her eyes and glared at him. "What I do in my off time is my business. Your house won't suffer because I write."

"What do you write?"

If she was a reporter set on a story, he'd kick her off the ranch so fast the new would rub off her boots.

"Books," she mumbled, her gaze dropping to his throat. She watched his pulse, fascinated to see its slow, steady beat against the hollow of his throat. She'd have to remember to use that in a scene.

"What kind of books?"

She didn't need this. She didn't need the laughter and derision she'd get. She was no stranger to it. Her own father laughed at her ideas. Marc had scoffed at her ambitions. But she firmed her resolve, refusing to allow her father, Marc or new boss to deter her.

"Romance novels," she said proudly.

Three

"*What?*" Josh took a step closer, his eyes blazing down at Molly. "You've come here to write *love stories?* Or is it research you are interested in? Stay away from my ranch hands! I don't want you doing any kind of *romance* research here. The first thing I know, I'll have a mutiny on my hands. You're here as housekeeper until I can get someone else. I should send you packing now."

"My imagination is much better than any reality. I don't plan to seduce any of your men. Does that make you feel better?"

She turned away, aware of the heat in her cheeks. She knew she was beet red and didn't need any more embarrassment. She also knew she shouldn't have mentioned romance books. Men all thought—

"No writing on my time."

"You don't need to worry, Mr. Hart. I have never..."

She trailed off. She'd planned to say she'd never had a problem with her work, but that wasn't strictly true. Her father constantly berated her for less than the perfection he sought. Her attempts to work in an office and the department store in the mall had met with far less than perfect results. Even the fast-food place had fired her. Scrupulously honest, Molly couldn't tell Josh Hart she never did less than outstanding work.

He didn't seem to notice her lapse.

"Call me Josh," he growled, heading for the door. "And see that you do your best."

He whipped it open and in seconds, Molly was alone. Slowly, she followed. The kitchen was empty. Crumbs on the plates indicated the men had eaten the sandwiches. She wondered if they had left anything for Josh.

He must have grabbed something or she was sure she'd have heard about it.

She wished they'd left her half a sandwich at least.

Molly cleared the table and did the dishes as her mind endlessly played over the scene in the study. She was determined to do the best job in the world for Josh Hart. He'd find nothing less than perfection, she vowed.

But her free time was her own and if she wanted to spend it writing romance novels, it was no one's business but her own.

After the scathing remarks Marc had made about her own abilities to attract and hold a man when he realized she was serious about ending their engagement, she didn't think she would ever fall in love again. When he'd asked her to marry him, she'd thought him a perfect mate. But her kisses didn't meet his standards; her own reluctance to go to bed before their marriage had confirmed his own belief that she had little sex appeal, and less attraction. It was clear when she discovered the reason for their engagement that he'd put himself out more than he expected.

But even now, seven months later, the pain of his words pierced sharp and direct.

So, facing reality, as her father constantly insisted, she knew better than to hope to find a man interested in her. Without his money, who did she think would want her?

Thinking she could appease her romantic nature by writing a book, a love story that would satisfy her own desires for a happy ending and offer some reading pleasure to others, she had started on her first book.

Imagination wasn't everything. She needed to draw from others. Her own experience was extremely limited and questionable now.

She'd have to find a way to cleverly work in any questions she had into conversations with the cowboys on the Rafter C. Maybe they'd unknowingly clue her in to what men really wanted in a mate, what they liked about women, beyond the obvious, and what they disliked about relationships.

She had plenty of material on what she as a woman disliked, from Marc. And her father. Enough to start, not enough to give her book the in-depth feeling she longed for.

The kitchen at last set to rights. She wiped her hands on the damp dishtowel, tossed it on the counter and headed for the door. There wasn't enough food in the place for dinner. If she was to shop for the evening meal, she'd better get going. Time was short and the distance to the nearest town considerable.

She headed to the barn, searching for Josh. How did

she buy the food? Did he have a charge account at the local store, or did he have to give her cash for the purchases? She had a list, of sorts. Hopefully she remembered everything she'd need over the next few days. She didn't have much experience in planning meals. It hadn't been important before. Her father always had a cook. Once she had a few minutes, she'd see about planning hearty meals out for at least a week at a time— to know what to buy and in what quantity.

The wind blew from the west, tossing her hair around her face, and bringing with it a mingled scent of horses, cattle, grass and fresh air. Molly took a deep breath, held it to savor the freshness. As she reached the barn, the fragrance of hay became strong. She liked the blended aromas, good and bad. They were a far cry from downtown Houston and automobile fumes.

"Can I help you, little lady?" One of the older cowboys came out from the tack room. Molly recognized him immediately as the one who had asked if she'd worked in a preschool. Her smile was hesitant.

"Actually, I'm looking for Mr. Hart. I need to go shopping for food and don't know where he likes to shop or how to pay for the food."

"Josh's out somewhere. The Rafter C has an account at the Shop 'N Shop on the edge of town. Talk to the manager before you shop and he'll ring it up on Josh's tab. All the housekeepers did that."

"Thanks. I'll be back for dinner."

If she had only known they needed food before she arrived, she could have shopped on her way to the ranch, rather than heading back to town the same day.

She backed her car around and faced the driveway just as Josh rode up. Pausing until he passed her, she watched as he sat on the big bay horse like he'd been born to the saddle, tall and easy, his long legs hugging the horse's sides. She couldn't help staring.

Whether he wanted it or not, whether he ever found out or not, he was going to be the role model for the hero of her book. Maybe not his personality—she wanted a kinder, gentler man. But his face was perfect—rough-hewn, taut and tanned.

She wished he didn't wear a hat. She'd like to see the golden glow of his thick, wavy hair in the sunlight again. His shoulders gave the impression they could carry the weight of the world. Some woman would be lucky to have him share her burdens one day. His hands were strong and capable. Capable of being tender, she acknowledged as she remembered his thumb rubbing gently across her palm.

And capable of bringing an awareness that didn't end. Her heart rate sped up at the memory of his hand holding hers.

Josh did not pass. He reined in and dismounted in one fluid motion right beside her. Molly rolled down the window.

"Leaving?" His voice was silky with satisfaction.

"Only to buy groceries. I'll be back in time for dinner," she replied sweetly, giving him a false smile while she seethed with frustration. She didn't understand why he wanted her to leave so much. She'd have thought he'd be so grateful to have someone do the housework and cooking, he'd make some effort to appease that person.

Her.

She wanted him to ask her to stay. To do something to show that she was special to him, if only to relieve him of the tasks around the house.

Special to him?

She didn't want to be special to anyone. She wanted to prove to herself and her father that she was capable of choosing her own life and living it the way she wanted. Maybe one day, in the far distant future, she'd find a man who would love her for herself, not for her sexiness, which she obviously lacked, not because she waited on him hand and foot. But just because of who she was.

And it was certain that that man would be nothing like Josh Hart. Though, she sighed softly, in all honesty he probably wouldn't approach Josh in the looks department either. Josh had to be the best-looking man she'd ever seen.

"What are you getting?" he asked.

"Do you want to see the list?" She snatched it up from the seat beside her and thrust it through the open window. Josh made no move to take it. His eyes glimmered as he stared down through the window. Shaded by his hat, they appeared as cool as a frosty foggy morning. But Molly had seen them flare hot and silver when angry.

"So you're coming back?" he asked.

"Yes! Honestly, do you think to drive me away with your less than welcoming attitude? You need me."

"And you're just a woman who wants to be needed."

Was that part of the determination of staying in a job where her boss obviously didn't want her? She wanted to be needed for the first time in her life?

She pulled her hand back, tossed the list beside her and put the car in gear. "I have work to do. As boss you can laze around if you want, but if I'm to get back in time to make dinner, I need to get going."

His teeth were white and even when he smiled at her bold speech. Molly took a deep breath and forced her eyes forward. Time enough later to build up resistance, if they wanted dinner at seven, she had to hurry.

Josh stood and watched as Molly maneuvered her car around the house and drove back down the driveway. A snippy thing. None of his other housekeepers sassed him like she did. He must be getting soft in the head since he allowed it.

Next time he'd remind her of the respect due the boss of a spread the size of the Rafter C. Remind her she was only here temporarily and if she wanted to stay even until the next housekeeper arrived, she had better watch her mouth.

It took Molly much longer to find the store than she anticipated. And buying everything on her list from a supermarket that was totally unfamiliar took even longer. Consequently, by the time she reached the Rafter C, it would be close to the dinner hour. Even then, she was pushing it.

She stopped at a take-and-bake pizza parlor and bought half a dozen large pizzas. Surely cowboys loved pizza. And living so far from town, they probably didn't get it often. As soon as she reached home, she'd pop them in the oven two at a time if she was lucky, while she unloaded her car. By the time she had the groceries put away, she hoped the pizzas would be ready to serve.

She didn't have time to prepare more. There were a lot of perishable groceries she'd have to put away at once after the car ride. Tomorrow she'd fix a full meal with a roast, baked potatoes, vegetables and biscuits.

Arriving at the Rafter C, Molly felt almost as if she were coming home. She hadn't even taken her suitcases from her car, yet the homestead welcomed her back as if she'd lived there for years.

No sooner had she stopped near the back door than Josh strode out of the house. He opened the passenger door and began to pull out grocery bags. Molly carried the pizzas inside and turned on the oven. The double ovens would come in handy; she'd be able to cook at least two pizzas at once.

"Took you long enough," he said as he dumped two bags on the long counter.

"I had trouble finding the right store. Then I had to wait while the manager finished talking with a sales rep to get the okay to charge the purchases. And then there was a lot to buy."

She headed back to unload other bags from her car, Josh at her side. Had he helped the other housekeepers? She didn't ask. It was enough that he helped her.

When the groceries had been unloaded, Josh

reached in the trunk for her two suitcases. "I'll take these to your room. It's at the top of the stairs on the right. Did you see it when looking over the house this morning?" he asked.

"Actually, I didn't have a chance to look over the place, I was too busy cleaning the kitchen. Just dump them inside the door, I'll find them after dinner."

If she were sleeping upstairs on the right, where did he sleep? Not in the bunkhouse, of that she was sure. She hadn't given the sleeping arrangements any thought. Not that it mattered. She was more than sure Josh Hart could contain any lust around her.

She quickly put up the frozen packages and the milk. The rest could wait until after dinner. Hurrying to set the table, Molly wanted everything to be ready when the men trooped in. She refused to give Josh anything to complain about.

She'd multiplied the ingredients for the salad by twenty but even as she was filling the largest bowl she could find with the lettuce, tomatoes, carrots and radishes, she wondered if it would be enough. Thankfully, she bought several different bottles of dressing—the cowboys could choose their own.

Promptly at seven, Josh walked into the kitchen just as a stream of cowboys entered from the back door. Molly wondered if there were a whistle somewhere that blew to let them know when mealtime arrived. They each introduced themselves. Molly tried hard to remember what name went with which face. By the fifth or sixth man, however, she knew it was a lost cause.

She drew the last of the pizzas from the ovens and

set them on the big table. Finding a sharp knife, she handed it to one of the younger cowboys—was his name Billy?—and asked him to start cutting. Then she offered ice tea, coffee, and milk for beverages.

The men were silent as they ate. In only moments, the pizzas were gone. They looked at her.

Molly looked around. She hadn't gotten a single piece.

The silence stretched out and her eyes flew to Josh. He leaned back in his chair, his fingers tucked into the front pockets of his jeans, his legs sprawled out before him as his eyes tracked her.

"Is something wrong?" she asked.

"No. We're just waiting for the rest," Josh said slowly, the glimmer of a smile touching his lips, his gray eyes narrowed as he watched her. Curious to know what she would do. Give up and leave? Or had she more stamina than that?

"The rest?" Molly's heart dropped. A quick glance around the table assured her she had not misread the situation. There had not been enough food. Again.

She swallowed. There was nothing else for dinner. She had thought several slices of pizza would be enough. She never ate more than two herself. God, what was she going to do? No one said a word; they all just stared at her. Panicked, she looked at Josh again. Her job depended on her doing the work to his satisfaction. On providing good service. Not on sending cowboys to bed hungry.

A painful blush started in her chest and spread to her neck, her cheeks. The heat swamped her as the moments stretched out endlessly, silently. She swallowed again, praying for a miracle.

It came when Josh shook his head and pushed back his chair. "Omelets. And biscuits. You can make biscuits, can't you?"

She nodded.

Josh opened the industrial-size refrigerator and tallied the eggs. "Jason, go to the bunkhouse and see how many eggs you have there. We have two dozen here, bring back two dozen more if you have that many. Is there any meat?"

"There's some ham left over from the other night," one of the men volunteered.

"Bring that, too," Josh ordered, already removing the eggs from the refrigerator.

Four dozen eggs? Molly was astonished. Then reason quickly took over. Of course, there were almost two dozen people to feed and she already knew these men ate more than she did. Lots more. She should have figured that out on her own, especially after lunch.

She moved to clear an area on the counter, and hunted for the flour. She'd make enough biscuits for each man to have a dozen. She would—

"Carl, you and Pete put away the rest of groceries. Trevor, you find the onions and cut them up. Jack grate cheese. Lance—"

"I'll take care of the coffee and condiments, boss," Lance interrupted, his eyes dancing in amusement. He cleared the trays from the pizzas and moved to the stove. "Dennis will hunt up some more vegetables and Steve can find the jam."

Reaching around Molly, the cowboy called Lance drew down the large bags of flour. "It won't take long, ma'am, to know how much we like to eat. The pizza was a good idea, there just wasn't enough. We could probably each eat a whole one," he said gently.

Josh glared at him and nodded toward the stove. Lance smiled, touched his forehead with two fingers in a mock salute and moved slowly away.

Molly wished the floor would open up and swallow her completely. At least she had something to do and the men hadn't complained about having to do their own cooking. Though she knew they must be mad as hornets. They'd worked hard all day and come to dinner expecting a hot meal. She'd fed them tidbits. Now they had to make their own suppers.

She darted a quick glance at Josh. He hadn't said a word of reproach.

In fact, he seemed to be surprisingly calm about the entire episode.

Yet she knew it would be reason enough to fire her. More than enough after lunch. No sense in waiting for the replacement that wouldn't come. He'd seen enough incompetence to fire her on the spot.

Molly ignored the rough teasing and laughter the men shared. She concentrated on making the biscuits, watching each batch cook to make sure they turned out perfect. She wanted to make amends, but wasn't sure how. She wanted to prove she could do this job, but wasn't sure she'd get another chance.

Josh seemed a hard man, not one given to forgiving repeated errors in judgment.

When the omelets had been cooked and the first two batches of biscuits were on the table, the men sat back down. Josh came across the room and placed his hands on her shoulders, turning her from watching the stove to push her toward the chair next to his.

"We have timers for that. Sit down and eat."

She shook her head. "I'm fine. I want to make sure the biscuits don't burn." She didn't deserve his kindness. She'd made a mess of dinner.

His hands pushed her down into the chair. They were warm and hard, and when he removed them, she felt a chill. He sat at the head of the table and nodded toward her plate, which had been piled high with a fluffy cheese, ham and vegetable omelet. One of the men tossed a hot biscuit on the plate and another poured her a cup of coffee.

"Eat," Josh ordered.

"Mrs. Montgomery said you were bossy," she muttered as she reached for some butter.

"She's got you pegged, boss," Lance said, giving a slow smile across the table to Molly. "What else did the employment agency say? We know Josh is hell on wheels with housekeepers. He hasn't kept one for longer than a couple of weeks."

Molly looked up, tempted to relate all Sarah Montgomery had said, but she held her tongue. Josh was her boss and deserved her loyalty.

She smiled and shook her head. "Just that he was bossy. Which makes sense since he is the boss, right?"

"You could add slave driver," Carl mumbled, his eyes on his plate.

"Or stubborn," Dennis threw in.

"How about opinionated?" Jack said slyly, throwing Josh a knowing look.

"I like relentless, myself," Pete said.

"And I like it quiet at dinner," Josh said, frowning.

When everyone laughed, Molly knew the men really liked and respected her new boss. It said a lot for him that the cowboys were comfortable enough around him to tease him. Something inside her reacted. She knew she still had to answer for the poor dinner, but maybe Josh would be generous and give her one more chance. She would not repeat the mistake of too little food again.

As the men ate, conversation centered on the ranch and the different tasks and chores still to be done.

Molly tried to match names to faces. Lance was the foreman. A man about the same age as Josh, he maintained just enough distance from the men to keep the chain of command, yet from the easy way the others related, he obviously was also well liked.

Jack was older, his hair liberally sprinkled with gray. Billy was the youngest and looked to Molly like he should still be in school. The others ranged in age and size, yet all had the same undefinable characteristic of a cowboy, a bit wild, a bit untamed, men in their own right who signed on to work the open land as their forebears had done a hundred years before.

Molly found them fascinating. She soaked up the conversation like a sponge. Afraid to ask questions, she tried to glean the meaning from everything without appearing stupid. Once or twice someone explained things to her, but for the most part, she had to guess at the meanings of some words.

When everyone had their fill of food and conversation, they began to drift out. Josh left first and Molly wasn't sure whether to be glad or not.

At least her reprimand would be delayed, or had he gone to write a check for her services and fire her? She hadn't done much her first day. She hoped she'd have more time.

She cleaned up the kitchen, checked where the cowboys had stored the food and tried to plan the next day's menu. Obviously she hadn't bought enough food to last a week. Still she had plenty for the next couple of days.

The first thing she planned to do when she hooked up her computer was make a list of groceries, of meals, of snacks. Then she would have a better idea of quantity amounts to order.

Finished with the dishes, she headed toward the stairs to find her room. She still hadn't seen Josh since dinner. Dare she unpack?

If he planned to fire her, wouldn't he have done so immediately after dinner? Or even as they were preparing the second part of the meal.

She paused in the doorway, her eyes taking in the pretty room. It was large, with high ceilings and tall windows, which gave a spectacular view of the rolling fields. Starched Priscilla curtains framed the view. Slowly she stepped inside. The bed was to one side, a dark burgundy coverlet adding a splash of color against the white walls. The rug in the center of the room gave beneath her feet when she walked on it. A dresser and a desk were on one wall. The closet door was ajar. And the adjoining bathroom guaranteed privacy. She'd be very comfortable here. It was much more than she expected.

As she opened drawers in the high chest, she wondered which room was Josh's. Hers was at the top of the stairs. There was a door opposite, and three more farther down the hall. Time enough to discover his when cleaning, changing beds, and the other tasks ahead of her.

If she stayed.

Molly put away the last shirt, snapped closed her two bags and shoved them under her bed. Turning, she heard Josh's tread on the stairs. Her door stood open so she could catch him when he came upstairs. She crossed her room reaching the opening to the hall just as he reached the top of the stairs.

He looked tired. Yet when he saw her waiting, he straightened and raised one eyebrow.

"I thought you might be asleep by now. Breakfast is at six," he said.

"I thought I might be fired by now."

He stared at her for a long moment. "No need. You're here temporarily. As soon as the agency finds someone else, you'll be gone. As you pointed out, I might as well take advantage of what you can do in the next few days."

"I plan on pancakes for breakfast, about fifteen for each man. Will that hold everyone?" she asked, disappointed by his continued conviction she would be so soon gone. Though in all fairness she'd hardly impressed anyone today.

He smiled and nodded. "Probably."

"I'm sorry I made such a mess with dinner. I thought two or three slices of pizza would be enough. I won't make that mistake again."

"Something else, no doubt," he murmured. His gaze roamed over her face, her hair.

"No doubt." She grinned. He was being nicer than she expected.

"Where did you get the pizzas?"

"At a take-and-bake place near the supermarket. I was running late and thought they'd do."

"They let you charge it?"

She shook her head. "I bought them."

Josh studied her for a long moment. "How much experience do you have being a housekeeper?" he asked, moving to lean against the wall, crossing his arms over his chest. Molly knew he'd stay for a while, so there was no hope a quick answer would turn him away.

Leaning against the doorjamb, she put her hands in her pockets and tried to find an answer that would be truthful, yet give him the comfort he needed to know she could do the job.

"I kept house for a number of years," she began slowly.

"For a dozen men?"

She shook her head. "Just one, actually. Though we often had guests."

"Your dad?"

She nodded.

"Where is he now?" Josh's eyes narrowed as she fidgeted in the doorway.

Molly felt the subtle change from polite questioning to inquisition. She wanted to say goodnight and shut the door, but couldn't without raising suspicions she wanted to avoid.

"He lives in Houston."

"Why did you take this job?"

Dare she hint at the reason? He probably sympathized with her father. He reminded her of her father, yet he was different. She didn't think her father would have come up with a plan for the evening meal when she failed to deliver. He would have sat back, waited for her to come up with something, then lectured her for hours on how inept she was.

Josh had not said a word. She almost wished he would. His kindness sat uneasily upon her. Boiling anger she was used to, kindness she was not.

Josh counted the minutes as she stalled, obviously searching for some answer to appease him. For a moment suspicions flared. He didn't want to be fobbed off with some politically correct response, he wanted to know why she was working as a housekeeper on a ranch miles from anything when she should be in some town, building a career, dating.

Frowning, he found he didn't like the idea of her dating, which was totally illogical. He didn't want to become involved with her or any woman. He'd tried that route with Jeannie and look at the heartache that had caused.

Nothing good came of women practicing their guile on unsuspecting men. He had a ranch full of single men and he didn't need some pretty young woman causing havoc. The sooner she left, the better.

"If it takes you as long to think up a plot for your book, you're going to be an old lady before you get the first manuscript done," he drawled sarcastically. Pushing away from the wall, he started down the hall.

"Get some sleep, 6:00 am comes early," he called over his shoulder.

When he entered the farthest door on the left, Molly sagged in relief. At least she'd made it through the first day.

Slowly she entered her room and shut her door. She was an idiot. Now that the moment had passed she realized she should have had all her answers ready. Why would someone want to keep house at the back of beyond? She didn't ride particularly well, nor care for horses that much. She knew nothing about cattle. And she knew even less about cowboys and their appetites.

But she still planned to remain for the duration. Tomorrow she'd get the house organized, set up her computer and begin working again on her book.

In the meantime she'd go to bed like Josh suggested and forget about the less than enthusiastic welcome she'd received.

And ignore the shimmers of attraction that played between them. He was her boss for the foreseeable future, nothing more. She was happy to keep things that way.

Not that it would hurt to just imagine how he would talk to her if he cared something for her. Not that it would hurt to imagine how his skin would feel beneath her fingertips, how his mouth would feel against hers, how his arms would feel holding her.

Shivering, she shook her head. It might not hurt, but it wouldn't change anything. She needed to be practical now. Her future depended on it.

By the time eighteen men had eaten breakfast and left for the day's work, Molly was almost ready for a nap. She'd risen early to prepare the meal. Pleased to note she had everything ready when the ranch hands filed in.

And she'd done it right.

There was plenty of pancakes, sausages, even a couple of eggs fried for Jack when he asked. She made two pots of coffee and had to quickly brew a third before they were filled.

Now the kitchen would take an hour or more to set right. And she still had to explore the rest of the house to make sure it was tidy before she could set up her computer.

Conscientious, she had to give her first efforts to her job. Her own time and projects had to wait.

Then she had lunch to see to and dinner to plan.

Sipping from a cup of lukewarm coffee, she wondered where all the free time was she'd expected. At the rate she was going, it would be the weekend before she even unloaded the computer from her car.

Determined to give her best to the job, however, Molly didn't hesitate to plunge right in. Once the kitchen was clean, she wandered through the downstairs rooms. On the wall in the big living room, family pictures clustered. She studied them. They showed a happy family frolicking in the snow, on a picnic somewhere, on horseback, mother, father, three children. Then only pictures of the children. She noted the progression as they all grew up. The most recent pictures showed new family groups. Obviously Josh's brother and sister were now starting families of their own. Why hadn't Josh married?

As if her thoughts of him conjured him up, he appeared in the archway to the hall.

"What are you doing?" he asked, tapping his hat against his thigh as he studied Molly's guilty expression when she whirled from the pictures.

"Just looking around. This room needs a thorough cleaning," she answered hurriedly. She didn't want him to know she'd been paying so much attention to a family that meant nothing to her. They'd looked so happy. Had she been that happy as a child? It was hard to think back when recent events still claimed her thoughts.

She was an only child of a difficult man. Her mother had left when she was a toddler, and her father had never spent time on picnics or playing with her in the snow. Josh had been lucky in his childhood and for a moment envy rose.

Four

"The whole place needs a thorough cleaning," he said, glancing around the room.

Molly nodded and stepped forward. He was tall. If she used him as the hero in her book, she should probably know exactly how tall he stood. Stepping closer, she noticed her head just reached his chin. His shoulders seemed even broader when she came close like this. Her hands itched to measure the width, to feel the hardness of his muscles, to sculpt their strength.

Tilting her head slightly, she wondered how hot his skin would feel. Would it be sleek and taut over his muscles? Or was his skin covered in hair? Golden hair covered his forearms, shining against the tan of his skin. Was he covered all over, or was his chest smooth and bare?

Swallowing hard, Molly tried to move her gaze away from the man. While her perusal was for research, she found herself warming at the thoughts running through her mind.

Slowly she drew in a shaky breath and tried to remember what she was supposed to be doing.

"Are you all right?" Josh's sharp voice penetrated the

haze and she swung around to face him.

"Of course."

"You look as if you've gone into a trance."

"I was thinking of something for my story."

He leaned forward a little until he was close enough that his breath brushed against her cheek when he exhaled. Entranced, Molly longed to reach up and touch his cheek, to trace the indentation beside his mouth, rub her fingertip across his lips and see if they were soft and warm, or hard and cool.

"I want a full day's work for a full day's pay," he said.

She blinked. "Why ever would you think you wouldn't get it? I'm a hard worker."

"You've been here twenty-four hours and so far you have practically starved us and done nothing else," he replied.

She grew indignant. "I cleaned your kitchen and went shopping for food, don't forget. Both were, I might add, a monumental task."

"Right, and by the amount of food you bought, you'll be heading out again tomorrow."

"Wait a minute. I wasn't aware of how much you would all eat. If you will recall, Mr. Hart, I offered to show you the list when I was leaving. If you had even glanced at it, you might have seen I was a little light on some of the supplies and let me know. So if I do have to go back tomorrow, I count you as much to blame as me."

Josh stared at her in disbelief. "You're blaming me for your own ineptitude?"

She tilted her chin, planted her fists on her hips and

nodded. "Not that I consider myself inept, just a bit inexperienced. Which you should have known."

"My dear Miss Forrester, I expect the agency to send me someone competent and capable, not someone who has to be led around like a two-year-old."

Glaring at him, she wanted to retaliate in words that would set him back on his heels. But nothing came to mind.

"I'm hardly a two-year-old. As soon as I get my computer hooked up, I'll make a master list and be sure to buy more than enough of everything I need the next time I go shopping."

A thought struck her. "But how I'll fit it all in my car, I'm not sure..."

She trailed off. Her car had been packed with groceries yesterday. If she bought even more, she'd need to make two trips.

"Take one of the ranch trucks. You can fill the pickup bed with the groceries. That's what the other housekeepers did."

She frowned. "I don't know if I can drive a truck."

"I'll get one of the men to show you how if you don't think you can manage."

"I'm sure I can manage." Her tone was haughty, her eyes still flashed anger.

"I'm sure you can."

His gentle tone grated. Dropping her gaze, she watched his lips move as he talked, and again wondered how they would feel against her own.

She had been kissed by different men and boys numerous times since high school. All the romance books she read made kisses sound like a most wonderful experience. She'd enjoyed kissing, but hadn't thought it was the most wonderful thing. Would Josh's kisses rock her world?

He'd shaved that morning and his cheeks looked smooth and warm. If he kissed her, would she feel more of his face against her own than just his lips? Would his arms encircle her to pull—

"Molly!"

She jumped. "What?"

He put a gentle fist beneath her jaw and raised her face until she met his gaze. His eyes narrowed as he stared down at her in displeasure, his expression serious.

"Do you need to go back to bed?"

To bed? With Josh?

She blinked again and tried to dispel the image his words evoked.

"Why would I need to go to bed?" Was he propositioning her? She had to refuse. Didn't she?

He groaned softly and his fist opened. His hand cupped her chin and the pad of his thumb traced the soft skin covering her jaw.

Molly shivered. She liked his touch. Her skin transmitted the sensuous sensations throughout her entire body and shimmering tingles of awareness rushed through. She had never felt like this before. Could she capture this feeling in her book, too?

"Molly, you look at me like I'm a long-awaited Christmas present. If you're making a play for me, forget it. I'm not interested. If this is research for your damn book, find someone else to practice on."

She jerked her head away and stepped back, embarrassment flooding her. "You told me to leave your employees alone."

"More importantly, leave me alone."

"I didn't do anything," she protested, knowing her imagination had been in full force but he couldn't know that.

"I guess not."

He straightened, slapped his hat against his thigh again and looked around the room, as if surprised to find himself there. "I came in to do paperwork. You need to tell me how much the pizzas cost. I'll reimburse you."

"No need. It is the least I can do after making such a mess of things yesterday."

"You don't need to buy us food."

"I don't mind."

"Molly, I pay for the food on the Rafter C."

"All right! The receipt's in my purse, I'll get it when I finish cleaning here."

"Fine. I have some laundry that needs doing, too."

"Of course, I'm here to serve," she muttered, feeling out of sorts. She needed to be alone to bring her rioting imagination under control.

"Just so you remember."

"What?"

"That you're here to serve. Not to go off on some writing tangent any time you feel the urge."

Writing wasn't the urge she felt right now. Hitting him over the head with a vase came close.

She tossed her hair and moved past him. "I know

what I'm here for, and don't think I won't do the best job you've ever seen."

"You have a way to go to prove that to me," he mumbled, slamming his hat on his head and striding across the hall to the office.

Molly acknowledged he had a point. So far her performance hadn't been very good. But she knew more now and wouldn't make the same mistakes twice.

She ran upstairs. While she cleaned the downstairs, she'd pop his things into the washer. Hesitating only a moment, she pushed open the door to his room. Glancing around curiously, Molly studied the masculine clutter. Clothes were piled haphazardly around. The bed, rumpled and unmade, drew her attention. For a moment, she imagined Josh stretched out on the dark sheets, a golden warrior resting before the next battle. Sunlight bright and bold bathed the room in clear light.

She moved to the piles of clothes and began to sort them for the wash. She could smell horses and dust and male sweat. Her heart kicked into high gear at Josh's scent. Strong, masculine, enticing, it kept her attention focused on him even when he was absent.

Frowning, she picked up the pile of jeans and headed downstairs. The washer and dryer were off the kitchen. She'd start the load, and begin to clean the living room.

Just maybe this job wasn't the perfect one to enable her to write, Molly admitted as she stood out of the way of the lunch stampede. She'd made thick roast beef sandwiches for the men, three large ones each. A huge fruit salad, which had taken every bit of fruit she'd bought just yesterday, and three bags of chips, graced the table, as well. She poured hot coffee as they began to eat.

Josh arrived a couple of minutes after the rest of them and flicked a glance to Molly as she scanned the table to make sure she'd prepared enough food this time.

"Coffee?" she asked as he sat at the head.

"Yes."

Josh sipped the hot beverage and stared at her over the rim of the cup. Flushed from the heat in the kitchen, Molly met his gaze, her eyes locked with his and she smiled before turning away.

He watched her cross the room, his gaze drifting down to the tight jeans that hugged her hips. He set his cup down with a thunk and glanced around at the men eating. Lance met his eye, looked back at Molly. Josh frowned—he didn't need any of the men getting distracted by Molly. He stared at Lance until the foreman met his gaze again and grinned.

Josh didn't need the distraction himself. Molly was his housekeeper until the agency sent another. Why they'd sent her in the first place was beyond him. And he didn't like it one bit. He wanted someone more suitable to ranch life.

When Molly sat down beside him and reached for a sandwich, he couldn't help noticing how gracefully she moved, how her hair gleamed in the kitchen light with threads of gold mingled with the brown. How her gaze moved shyly around the rough cowboys, and how easily she replied to their remarks.

For a moment, the old anger surfaced. Jeannie had charmed everyone, flirted with everyone until he'd almost exploded. When he called her on it, she'd act all hurt and upset. It had all been a game to her. One with disastrous consequences.

He studied Molly, annoyed to find her attitude more friendly than flirtatious. Her wide-eyed curiosity about ranch life appealed to the men and they were knocking themselves out to explain everything to her.

Molly felt Josh's eyes on her but ignored him. She gave every appearance of listening to what Pete told her about shoeing horses on the range. But her attention split, only one part really listened, the other tried to figure out her reaction to Josh Hart every time he came near her.

It was odd, but she felt somehow attuned to him. She knew when he watched her, could feel the attention like a touch. She wished she dare turn and meet his gaze, hold it until he looked away first.

An imp of mischief took hold. Maybe she'd have to prove to him that she wasn't interested in him. Maybe playing up to one of the cowboys—

Lance caught her eye, his studying her. He flicked a quick glance to Josh, back to Molly, a slow grin starting. Molly flushed. Had he read her mind? When he winked at her, she looked away. Too bad she didn't feel the same attraction to Lance. He was handsome, tough with the men, yet had a sensitivity about him that she found immensely appealing. However, no attraction simmered between them, not like she felt with—

"If you'd like, you can come with me this afternoon," Lance said easily. "I can show you some more of the ranch."

"She has work to do here," Josh growled, frowning at his foreman. "I pay her for housework, not to keep you company while you work."

Lance grinned and shrugged. "Sure thing, boss. I just thought Molly might like to see some of the ranch, that's all. You know, have her get to know the place she now calls home."

"She's not going to be here long enough to call this home," Josh said, glaring at Molly.

The men stopped eating and stared at Josh, then Molly. Slowly, one by one, they looked at each other. Conversation lagged for several minutes, before picking up again.

Molly glared at him. There was no need for him to announce to the entire table that she wasn't wanted.

She started to say something, thought better of it and snapped her mouth closed. If the reports from the agency were to be believed, Josh was going to have a long wait to find a replacement.

And while she didn't plan to stay forever, she wanted to leave on her terms, not his.

She smiled at Lance. "Thanks for the offer. Maybe on my day off."

Throwing Josh a challenging look, she dared him to deny she would have some free time. No matter how hard a boss he proved, everyone got time off.

"I'll take you around on your day off, if you want to see the rest of the ranch," Josh said, reaching for the coffeepot and refilling his cup.

Molly thought she'd enjoy seeing the ranch with Lance, but wasn't so sure about going with Josh. Maybe she could get him to unbend a little before her day off so the day wouldn't be awkward. Did he ever laugh and joke like the other men did? What did he do with his off time?

With lunch over, Molly returned to cleaning. She made inroads in the living room and wanted to finish before starting dinner. The room had been neglected for too long. She had dusted everything, cleaned the pictures, and vacuumed the rug, floor and furniture. She wanted to wash the windows so the room would sparkle. There was something very satisfying about bringing order out of chaos. She liked knowing she was making a difference in the room, in the house. To the men.

Josh had gone into his office to work after lunch and Molly heard his voice from time to time on the phone. Getting the window cleaner and a roll of paper towels, she began the final task in the room. As she worked, her gaze was drawn time and again to the rich green grass of the range that spread out before her. In the far distance the dark outline of the distant mountains rose from the high plains. They seemed to absorb the sunlight.

She saw the trees near the house sway in the wind. This would be a perfect setting for a romance novel. She could describe the lushness of the ranch. Maybe have her heroine and hero get lost in the vast range. She frowned. No, that wouldn't work, the hero would know his way around and—

"Molly?"

She turned. Josh stood inches away. She hadn't heard him come in.

"Yes."

"What are you doing?"

"Washing windows." What did it look like she was doing?

"You haven't moved a muscle in minutes. I watched you."

She shook her head and turned back to the window. The cleaner had run and dried. She'd been daydreaming again. Guiltily, she sprayed the cleaner on again and wiped hard to eradicate the streaks. "Was there something you wanted?"

"I realized after lunch that we hadn't discussed your days off. I thought the usual ones of Saturday and Sunday."

"What about meals for the men on those days?" she asked.

Embarrassed, she worked while she talked. She didn't want him to fire her for daydreaming. Three times before was enough.

"We can get our own. Even when Rachel was here, she didn't cook every day."

"I don't mind cooking, if you want. If I can write the rest of the day. I don't have any place else to go," she said.

"Most of the men take off for town on Saturdays. You might make something ahead for Sunday dinner that we can heat up."

She nodded, every inch of her body aware of Josh's proximity. Diligently, she sprayed another pane, began to wipe it clean. Distracted with her reactions around him, she tried to cover her feelings. She'd die if he ever suspected her interest.

"What were you doing when I came in?" He refused to let it go.

"I guess I was thinking about the ranch. It's pretty here. You can see the mountains in the distance; between here and there all the range is green with grass. I can just see some cattle on that rise to the left."

"The room looks nice," he said almost grudgingly.

He had work to do. He didn't have time to hang around his housekeeper while she washed windows. Glancing around, he noticed how tidy she'd made everything; even the pictures on the walls sparkled.

She was right, when she worked, she proved to be a hard worker. But he knew she'd been a million miles away when he'd walked into the room.

"The pictures are of your family?" Molly asked when she turned to see if he had left and found him staring at the photographs.

"My brother and sister. My folks died when we were young."

"I'm sorry. Do your brother and sister live near here?"

"Brianna lives in Texarkana where she teaches at the local college. Jase and his wife have a spread in west Texas."

"So he's a rancher, like you?"

Josh turned to face her, his face impassive. "He's always been a rancher. He kept us together with him after our folks died. He really raised Brianna and me. The Rafter C belongs to all of us, not just me."

"But you run it."

"Yeah, I run it."

"Very successfully, I'd say," Molly said with a smile.

Josh's expression hardened. Tension filled the room. "Well enough," he retorted.

Molly wondered what she'd said wrong. Most people liked being complimented on doing something well.

She had been about to congratulate herself on managing a conversation for several minutes without Josh getting angry. Obviously she'd said something to touch him off, but what?

"Let's get one thing clear up front," he said, glaring down at her. "This is a family ranch. I don't own it all. And I have no intention of sharing it with anyone. Especially someone as flighty as you."

Molly stared at him. Was he nuts?

"Excuse me, did I miss something in the conversation? I don't want to share this ranch with you. I'm here to work. When I finish my book, I'm going to move back to town and get an apartment of my own and never have to answer to anyone again."

"Right."

She fumed at his sarcastic tone. Boldly she stepped closer and jutted her chin up at him. "Listen to me, Mr. Hot-Shot Rancher, I'm not making a play for you or any other man. I'm focused on my new job and my goal to write a novel. I'm certainly not making a play for a bossy, arrogant rancher who can't even keep a housekeeper for longer than a month!"

"He either did a number on you or you're trying to do one on me," Josh drawled.

"I'm not trying to do anything on you. I'm here to keep house, nothing more."

"And write your book," he added slyly.

"That, too."

"I've seen women use their wiles to try to get their way. I'm not susceptible this time around," he warned.

Outraged, Molly slammed her fists on her hips and stepped even closer, until she could feel the radiant heat from Josh's body, until she could smell Josh's scent.

"Forget it, cowboy. I've had my fill of domineering, bossy, arrogant men. My father was one, my ex-fiancé was one. You would be my last choice, even if I considered getting involved."

"Good, just so we understand each other." He paused a heartbeat, then relaxed a fraction. "I was engaged once myself. To a woman who only wanted the ranch and the perks the money could buy."

She blinked, her anger fleeing instantly. Behind the evenly spoken words, Molly recognized the hurt and disillusion he'd die if he knew he'd revealed. No wonder he suspected her. His experience with the opposite sex didn't appear to be any better than hers.

"Well, don't paint me with that brush. I don't want your ranch, your money or you."

Liar.

Her conscience whispered how much she would like to know him better. See where the sensual pull that played each time she drew near would lead. Clamping down on those thoughts, she forced herself to keep her stance.

Josh stared at her and wished he could say the same thing. He didn't trust her any farther than he could throw her, but he wanted her.

Suddenly every instinct he owned honed in on the slender woman standing so boldly before him. He hadn't felt like this since he'd discovered Jeannie's betrayal.

He didn't like it. He had no intentions of getting tangled up with this bit of fluff just to ease an itch. Lust he could control. And there was nothing else between them.

"—with Lance."

"What?"

"I said there's no need to show me the ranch on the weekend, I'll go with Lance."

"Like hell you will. I'm the boss of the spread, and I don't want you and Lance mixing it up. If you need to see the ranch, I'll take you."

"Well, we wouldn't want to think I'm making a play for you, would we?"

She smiled up at him with so much mockery in her look he wanted to wipe the expression off her face. His hands fisted at his sides and he found it almost impossible to remain where he stood.

"I'd know."

Her smile faltered for a split second, then she upped the wattage. "I'm sure you would, cowboy. You probably have women coming on to you all the time. Gets old, does it?"

"Nothing I can't handle." Slowly he relaxed his hands, stepped closer, his eyes narrowed with intent.

She stepped back.

"Too late, sugar," Josh muttered as he reached out and slid his hand beneath the silky hair to the nape of her neck. His mouth came down on hers.

Molly opened hers to shriek a stop, but she was too late, just as he had said. His lips covered hers in a searing kiss.

Scalding heat swept through her. Pulsating blood pounded, tingling awareness focused on the man holding her for his kiss. His lips moved against hers in an erotic dance that shimmered through every nerve ending. When his tongue made a brief foray into the dark cavern of her mouth, Molly moaned softly in unexpected delight.

She was greedy, she admitted. She wanted more.

Moving closer, she was shocked when her body came into contact with his. His other arm encircled her and drew her into the tight embrace against his rock-hard length. His chest was solid against her softness, his legs strong enough to support them both. She put her arms around his back, feeling the heat through his shirt, tracing the strong corded muscles.

On fire, burning up from within, Molly couldn't breathe, couldn't hear anything with the blood pounding wildly through her veins. She could only feel.

It was as good as the books hinted. Better.

Josh eased back, his hands on her shoulders now, his eyes hooded and watchful. Molly slowly lifted her lids and gazed at him, knowing her feelings must show, unable to summon the strength to hide them.

"A scene for your book?" he asked huskily.

Instantly she dropped her hands and turned away, curiously hurt. Had the kiss meant nothing to him? Had she been the only one to feel anything?

"Maybe," she replied.

Damage control, however late, was definitely in order. She raised her head, threw back her shoulders and marched over to the windows to continue cleaning. She hoped passionately that he couldn't see how weak her knees still felt, how her heart hammered in her chest, how the blood still sang with the memory of his touch. She licked her lips and tasted him. Cravings filled her. She wanted more. And knew any more would be dangerous beyond belief.

"I'll apologize if you want," he said gruffly.

"Whatever for? A kiss is nothing. You've made your position clear and I hope I have, too. We have nothing each other wants and I'll stay away from you. You stay away from me." She was proud of her voice. It didn't shake.

After several moments of silence, Molly chanced looking over her shoulder. Josh had gone.

Slumping down in the nearest chair, she lightly rubbed her lips with her fingertips, reliving every second of their kiss. For someone who didn't like her, he did a credible job of kissing.

Much to her dismay, Molly wasn't able to toss off the kiss as she wanted. Its memory resurfaced time and time again as she worked during the afternoon.

She'd be dusting a table and the next thing she knew she found herself staring off into space, remembering Josh's touch, remembering how she felt when his lips moved against hers, when his body pressed into hers. It was nothing at all like Marc's kisses. And nothing as tame as the ones she'd read about in books.

Shaking her head, she'd return to her task, only to

find herself thinking more about the kiss than the work she had to do.

Giving up in exasperation, she stormed into the kitchen to prepare the evening meal. Maybe that would take her mind off Josh Hart and his killer kiss.

Stirring a batch of mashed potatoes when Lance sauntered into the kitchen, all cowboy charm, Molly looked up and smiled. No hidden undertones here. He was a male on the prowl and they both knew it.

"Howdy, darlin'. Need any help?" he asked, leaning against the kitchen counter crowding her, watching her.

"You can set the table if you want."

It soothed her pride that he flirted with her. At least one man on the ranch wasn't anxious for her to leave.

"Could. Maybe I was just being friendly and wanted to watch you work."

"Get a charge out of watching others work, huh?" She grinned at him. He was nice and friendly. Not like some men she could mention.

"Beats working myself."

"Actually, you could do me a favor, if you wouldn't mind?"

"Anything, darlin'."

Molly flushed at his flirting. She wasn't used to it and didn't know how to respond. "I haven't had a chance to finish taking the boxes out of my trunk, including my laptop. Maybe you could bring it all in for me and take it up to my room?"

"Sure." He nodded. "Where are your keys?"

"In my purse, on the dresser in my bedroom. It's the room at the top of the stairs."

"I'll find them."

Moving away, his boots stomping slightly on the wooden floor, Lance went to find her keys.

Molly put the potatoes back on the stove to keep warm and checked the biscuits. They were perfect, just a minute or two away from being done. She closed the oven door and turned to get the plates and silverware for the table.

She heard the rumble of masculine voices and stopped to listen.

"What the hell are you doing coming from Molly's room?"

Josh's voice.

Her heart dropped. Tossing everything on the table, she ran out into the hall.

"—keys so I can unload her car."

"She ask you?"

"As a matter of fact, yes." Lance's eyes danced in amusement as he faced off against Josh.

Molly halted when she reached them. A person would have to be dead to miss the tension that filled the hallway. The two men were of a size. They looked ready to fight at the drop of a hat.

"Is there a problem?"

She didn't want to be there, but if she was the cause, no matter how unknowing, she thought she should do something to ease the situation.

Josh shook his head and held out his hand to Lance. "I'll get her stuff."

Lance hesitated a moment, glanced at Molly and winked. "Fine." He dropped the keys into Josh's outstretched hand. "Guess I'll be setting the table, after all."

Josh looked at him sharply.

Lance shrugged, grinned, and headed back toward the kitchen. "I offered my services to Molly. She had a couple of suggestions."

Josh reached out and snagged Molly's arm as she turned to follow Lance. She looked up, surprised. Shimmering waves of excitement hit her and she wondered for a foolish moment if he planned to kiss her again.

"Lance is my foreman, not some kitchen help."

"He offered."

"What other services did he offer?"

Josh grit his teeth. He didn't care. He couldn't care. But he also couldn't walk away from her until he knew.

What else had Lance offered?

Five

Before Josh could say another word, Molly whirled around and rushed to the kitchen. She snatched up the hot pad and opened the oven door. The smell of burnt bread filled the kitchen just as the cowboys began to troop in.

One groaned.

Molly turned, her face stricken, holding the large cookie sheet of biscuits. Dumping the sheet on the counter, she flipped one biscuit over; its bottom was scorched. Turning, she glared at Josh as he followed her into the kitchen.

"This is all your fault, Josh Hart," she said, scraping them off the pan.

"You should have set the timer," he said, coming up behind her. Reaching around her, he scooped up one and examined the black bottom.

"Ha. I was doing fine until you caused me to forget cooking."

She began to place biscuit dough on a second cookie sheet. "I was watching them. I had everything under control until you started berating Lance for being in my room."

Instant silence filled the kitchen.

Molly closed her eyes and stifled a groan. Shaking her head, she resumed placing the cut biscuit dough on the cool pan. She'd watch this batch without distraction and make sure it didn't burn. No matter what Josh got up to, she'd concentrate on cooking.

"Pete, start dishing up. Not that it's the business of any of you, but I went to her room to get her car keys to unload the rest of her things," Lance said, calmly reaching for the platter of ham.

"And then you had to jump to conclusions and make a fuss," she whispered to Josh, trying to avoid the interested stare of the men seated around the table.

"What was I to think, seeing a man come from your room?" he whispered in return, his back to the men.

"Think whatever you want, just don't jump to conclusions about me. You'll probably be wrong."

She turned and almost bumped into him. Placing her hand on his chest, she pushed. It was like trying to move a mountain.

"You're in my way," she said.

"I knew you'd be a problem."

"I'm not the problem! If you hadn't gotten so upset with Lance over nothing, none of this would have happened," she snapped back.

"While you're here, I'm responsible for you. Think of me as in loco parentis."

"Give me a break! I have no need for a father, thank you very much. I'm old enough to live my own life the way I want. Move!"

Josh slowly stepped aside and watched as she

stormed over to the stove and grabbed the coffee. He peeled the bottoms off the last biscuits and tossed them into the basket, setting it in the center of the table.

He sat at the head and heaped his plate with the ham and mashed potatoes and green beans Molly had prepared.

There was plenty of food for everyone. Feeling proud of the fact, Molly took the vacant chair next to Josh and began to serve herself. No complaints about going hungry this night. It would have been perfect if the biscuits hadn't burned.

She glanced up at the odd expressions on the faces of the men. One by one they took a bite of potatoes, and then looked puzzled. Billy added salt and pepper to his, took another bite. His gaze slid across the table and met hers. Smiling gamely, he cut a hunk of ham.

"What did you do to the potatoes?" Josh's angry voice interrupted her musing.

She looked at him.

"Nothing. They're boxed. I planned on baked potatoes, but forgot to put them—"

He didn't need to hear she'd forgotten to put them in the oven in time and had to resort to boxed ones.

"We eat mashed potatoes all the time. They never taste like this."

She scooped up some and sampled. They were sweet! Suddenly she remembered, she'd been thinking how her heroine would never be caught in a kitchen in her story. Had she been daydreaming again and picked up sugar instead of salt to season the potatoes? Oh, good grief, couldn't she get one single meal right?

"They do taste a bit odd. Maybe the drying process altered the taste or the milk started to go bad."

There wasn't enough money in Texas to get her to confess before all these men that she had been so stupid to put sugar instead of salt into the mashed potatoes.

Josh stared at her.

Nervously Molly took a sip of ice tea and prayed he wouldn't attack her in front of everyone.

"Shall I make a fresh batch?" she asked just as the buzzer rang for the oven.

Grateful for the respite, she jumped up and withdrew the golden biscuits. Sighing with relief that these turned out perfectly, she gave each man two.

"We'll make it through with these, but maybe next time you should taste them before serving them," Josh said.

"Good idea."

She smiled brightly, more with relief than anything else, and sat back at her place.

"Odd potatoes or not, boss, this beats us cooking," one of the men said.

Josh had to agree with him.

As housekeepers went, Molly was the worst cook he'd seen. But she kept trying, he had to give her that.

And she was the easiest on the eyes. In fact, she looked downright pretty.

He frowned and forced his gaze away. She was too pretty for the ranch. He remembered his mother. He'd always thought she was the most beautiful woman in the world. He remembered more how loving she had always been, how there had been cookies and milk every day.

How she'd baked pies and cakes for the men—because her husband loved sweets.

He never saw her spend time on her hair or her makeup. But she'd always looked glamorous to him.

And she'd been content on the ranch. He never remembered her wanting to go out in the evenings. But he did remember playing games in the evenings, picnics out near where the cattle were when they were too far from home for his dad to come in for lunch.

Her life had been complete on the ranch with her family.

The tragedy of the automobile accident that claimed both her and his father had altered things forever.

He'd thought to find a woman just like her. And believed he had with Jeannie.

She had been pretty as a picture. And his former fiancée had stayed at the ranch several times. Her yearnings to go into town, or Dallas or Galveston he'd put down to not being fully part of the ranch. Which he expected to change when they married.

He should have read the signs. She liked parties, nightclubs and dancing. And pretty clothes. Clothes totally unsuitable to ranch life.

He flicked a glance to Molly as she ate quietly. At least Molly made an effort to dress appropriately. She'd worn tennis shoes today instead of her new boots, but the jeans and cotton shirt were suitable, if a bit snug.

Not that clothes alone made a woman suitable for ranch work.

Not that ranch work was what Miss Molly Forrester wanted. She considered herself a *writer*.

He wondered when she thought she'd find the time to actually sit down and write. Especially if she kept the house up to the standards she set with the living room and kitchen.

"Nice dinner, ma'am, despite the potatoes," Jack said, pushing back his chair.

"And the biscuits. The second batch came out good," Billy said.

Molly smiled, hoping the heat in her cheeks didn't show. She grew more and more determined to improve her cooking. Breakfast had been perfect. Lunch went well for the men who had been close to the house. Why had she let her mind wander when she cooked dinner?

"I still say it beats me having to cook," Lance added, tilting back in his chair and sipping from the cup of hot coffee. He smiled at Molly, his eyes studying her.

"It was good," Trevor said as he rose and headed out.

"Mighty fine, ma'am."

"Good night."

One by one the men left the house until only Josh and Lance remained at the table.

Josh looked at Lance. "Had enough?" he asked.

The foreman looked at him and raised his cup. "Still working on this one, boss. But you don't have to stay, Molly can keep me company."

"She has work to do," Josh replied.

"When I finish eating," she said, taking the last bite of ham. She'd pushed her potatoes around but eaten very little. At least she wouldn't make that mistake twice.

"Plenty of food tonight," Lance said. He glanced at

Josh and then smiled at Molly. "You go shopping again?"

"Nope, I called the store and they delivered. They even brought the groceries right into the kitchen. Saved me oodles of time."

"That's how you play housekeeper?" Josh asked.

"Don't knock it. I'm the best bet you have for housekeeper." Molly rose and began stacking the empty plates.

"Doesn't say much," Josh said.

"You're the one who drove the others off."

"Is that what Mrs. Montgomery told you?" he asked, tilting back in his chair, his hands tucked into the front slash pockets of his jeans.

Molly paused a moment, her eyes feasting on him. Then she resolutely moved to the sink.

"Yes."

"So we have you to blame, boss?" Lance said, setting down his cup, and rocking back in his chair.

"Let's see, when Rachel first left, it took two weeks to replace her. Her name was Alice. She was allergic to hay. I guess since I insisted we keep hay on the ranch for the animals I could be accused of running her off."

Lance nodded, smiling. "I remember her. She was the one sneezing all the time."

Molly tried not to smile while she ran water into the sink.

"And number two?" she asked, intrigued by this unexpected playful side of her austere boss. Especially after a less than perfect meal. Her father would have been ranting and raving for hours at her ineptitude.

"Ah, number two came a week later. Ms. Patricia

Dare. Only she dared nothing. She didn't like the isolation, didn't like being so far from town, didn't like the language of the men, didn't like the wind blowing constantly."

"Didn't like our wearing boots inside, didn't like our putting our hats on the backs of our chairs. She mostly didn't like anything," Lance added.

"I didn't notice any bad language," Molly said.

"Wait a few days. They're on the best behavior around you. It'll wear off when they're hot and tired and grumpy."

She slid her eyes toward him. "I've seen you grumpy and not heard anything so bad." Giving up the thought of washing the dishes for a few minutes, she turned off the water and leaned her back against the sink looking at the two cowboys.

Josh grinned and her heart flopped over. Unable to move her gaze, she could only stare and feel more alive than ever in her life. What was it about Josh?

He had two eyes like everyone else. Well, maybe his were more sexy than a man had a right to have, especially when he narrowed them to gaze down at her.

He had a nose and a mouth like everyone else. But unlike anyone else, his mouth had kissed her silly. Her body grew warm with the memory.

"That's because I'm on my best behavior, too. Sugar in the potatoes notwithstanding, having you is better than us fixing our own meals."

"I wouldn't have burned the biscuits if you and Lance hadn't been having words," she said primly. She had hoped he wouldn't mention the potatoes. She should have known better.

"We weren't having words, I simply asked what the hell he was doing in my house coming from your room." Josh's grin faded and he looked annoyed. "Next time you need help, ask me."

"Wasn't any trouble for me," Lance interjected.

Josh glared at him. "Don't you have some final chores to do tonight?'

"Nope." Lance looked at Josh in amusement. "I could stay here all night in fact."

"I could have managed to bring in all my things. Lance offered, so I thought I'd take him up on it. What's the big deal?"

"Yeah, boss, what's the big deal?"

Josh fished the keys from his pocket and tossed them to Lance. His foreman caught them easily.

"Then go get them. Burning biscuits prevented me from doing so."

Lance rocked down on all four legs of the chair and stood. Grabbing his hat from the back, he put it on. "I'll bring it all up to your room, Molly. Like I said I would earlier."

"Thank you. The laptop can go on the small desk in the room."

"There's more room in the office. You can use the second desk near the window, "Josh said. The light's better there than in your room."

"I don't want to be in your way."

"You won't have time to be in the office during the day. I do most of the office work during normal business hours. We won't conflict. If I have to work at night, you'll just have to put up with my presence."

Which would probably prove so distracting she wouldn't get a single word written. She knew her imagination would fly if Josh were nearby, but in the right direction?

Somehow she was beginning to see herself as the heroine to his hero. And that was never going to happen.

"Thank you."

"I'll get it now," Lance said heading outside.

"I'll be in the office," Josh said, rising and walking in that direction.

So much for there being no conflict in the evenings if she wanted to write then.

As Molly did the dishes, she thought maybe Mrs. Montgomery stretched the truth a bit. Josh hadn't proved impossible—yet. He'd certainly told her off a couple of times, but he had the right of it each time.

And he hadn't said much about dinner's disaster.

He'd given her more chances than the other places of employment had, and that was definitely in his favor. She wished he had continued telling her about the other housekeepers. If the first two left for the reasons he'd given, it didn't make him a demanding boss at all.

Why had the others left so soon after arriving?

Too tired to be creative by the time Molly had her computer hooked up, she opened the file of chapters she'd already written and read through them, editing as she went.

She didn't know where Josh had gone and refused to admit to being disappointed he didn't have work in the office that night. The lighting was good. And it was quiet. Maybe too quiet. Not that she wanted him there. What if he asked about her book, asked to read it to him?

Starting at chapter one, she found herself dissatisfied with the descriptions. They didn't really capture the essence of what she wanted to portray.

She closed her eyes imaging Josh standing beside her. How could she get that description down on paper so all readers would see him as she did?

Her head nodded.

She opened her eyes. She had to get to sleep if she was to get up early enough to prepare breakfast. With a sigh, she turned off the computer. Two days and not a single new word written. She might have underestimated how much time it would take to finish the book.

Molly felt as if her head had barely touched the pillow when loud, rapid knocking on her door woke her from a deep sleep. Sitting upright in surprise, she realized dawn was still a half hour away.

"Molly, dammit, wake up!" Josh pounded on her door and called her name. Was there a fire?

She scrambled from the bed and ran to the door, flinging it open. Blinking in the bright hall light, she peered up at him.

"What's wrong?"

He slowly lowered his still-raised hand as he took in her appearance. Her hair, tousled and disheveled from sleeping, swirled around her face like a soft brown cloud. A sleep crease from her sheet slashed across her cheek.

Her eyes were half closed against the light. And she wore a pale blue, skimpy satiny sleep shirt that draped over her, hugging her curves and valleys.

Josh felt a burst of desire unexpected and hard. He stepped closer, skimming the back of his fingers down her flushed, warm cheek.

"Is there a fire?" she asked, shaking her head to come awake.

"No fire."

His gaze traveled down to her pink polished toes. Her legs were bare, tanned, shapely. The sleep shirt, stopping at the midpoint of her thighs, almost fell off one shoulder.

"Josh?" Molly took in his attire. He wore only a terry robe. At least she thought that was all he wore. She could see his bronzed chest in the deep vee of the short robe; his muscular legs were bare. Why was he here? Why had he banged on her door like there was an emergency?

He leaned over and kissed her. Startled, Molly slipped her hands up to his shoulders to keep her balance. Then it seemed logical to encircle his neck, thread her fingers through his damp hair. His face was clean-shaven, no scratchy beard against her skin.

Wait. Damp hair, shaved?

Somewhere it registered that he'd already had his shower and probably wore nothing beneath his robe.

As she wore nothing beneath her shirt.

"Molly." He pulled back, breathing hard. "Where are my clothes?"

"What?"

She snapped open her eyes and stared at him. "What

do you mean, where are your clothes? In your—oh no!"

Whirling, she raced down the stairs and into the kitchen, flicking on the lights as she made her way through the house heading for the laundry room. Oh no, oh no oh no, she chanted, flinging up the lid to the washer. There in damp array sat his jeans and dark shirts. The pile of colored shirts were still on the floor next to the washer. Whites piled next to them.

She'd forgotten to put the jeans in the dryer yesterday! On the floor before the washer sat the other loads of clothes, all waiting to be washed.

"Damn!" Josh had followed her and stood in the doorway, his gaze immediately recognizing the situation.

"I can dry them right away." She pulled the heavy damp denims from the washer and stuffed them into the dryer.

"Denim takes forever to dry."

"Nonsense, they'll be dry by the time you finish breakfast," she said, crossing her fingers as she hit the On button. Putting soap into the washer, she scooped up another load and started that, as well.

"If you think I'm going to breakfast dressed like this, you're crazy," he said.

She looked at him and her heart melted. Her knees grew weak again and she held on to the washer like a lifeline.

He looked like he just got up from bed. His hair was mussed from her own hands. His eyes glittered at her and in the uncertain light, it looked like he wanted her. Which just proved her imagination worked even first thing in the morning.

She pushed away.

"I'm sorry. I guess I was so caught up in cleaning, I forgot to change the loads. I'll make sure they are all done today."

"Can you keep your mind on it?" he asked with an edge in his tone.

"Yes."

He had a right to be angry. It took less than twenty seconds to load the dryer and push the button. Why hadn't she thought once about the clothes after she'd gathered them from his room?

Maybe that kiss had had something to do with forgetting everything.

It would have been so easy if she'd put the clothes in to dry before going to bed.

She should have remembered!

"You'll excuse me for wondering. How could you forget something so simple?" he asked.

"I just did, okay? It won't happen again."

"I'm putting my money on that it will happen again. Molly, you're one strange woman. You go off into your own little world so far the house could burn down around you and I don't think you'd notice."

"So this housekeeper might be the one that just wandered away in her mind?" she joked, trying to ease the tension that shimmered between them.

"No, sweetheart, this one might be the one I fire," he said slowly.

"Please don't, Josh. I'll do better, I promise. It's just my way of coping."

"Coping with what?"

"My dad. He...nothing I did ever pleases him. He wants me to be accomplished like my mother. She left him when I was little. Left us both. So I don't even have a role model. He's a hard man, expects perfection. So I'd imagine I did things his way. That he liked what I did."

Loved me, she wanted to say, but stopped short before revealing that.

"And imagined a lot of other things to make life more bearable?" he asked with pinpoint accuracy.

She nodded. "But things are different here. I'm doing a good job. I know I've messed up a little—"

He laughed. "You've messed up more than anyone I've ever known. I'd hate to see your definition of messing up a lot!"

"But I'm getting better. I know now to fix tons of food. I won't put sugar in the potatoes again. I'll use the timer so I don't burn things. I've already cleaned the living room and hall. And I'll finish up the rest of the house before you know it."

"You're here temporarily, Molly. I told you that from the first, so don't get settled in too much."

"I know."

Once she sold her book, it wouldn't matter. She could live wherever she wanted. And write full time.

Still, it hurt just a little that he kept reminding her the assignment was only temporary.

"I'll be in the office. Bring my breakfast there," he said. Glancing down the length of her, he met her eyes. "And I suggest you change before starting breakfast or you'll have a dozen cowboys over you like flies on honey."

"Only a dozen?" she asked provocatively. Was he immune to her? Even after kissing her? Or was it because he'd kissed her and found her lacking?

He reached out and rubbed the pad of his thumb gently over her lower lip. "I think Jack's immune, too old. And a couple of the men have girlfriends. That leaves the rest of us."

She trembled at his touch, at his words. He'd included himself in the group of cowboys. It warmed her heart like nothing ever had.

"What a kind man you are," she said.

"Kind?"

"To say such a nice thing. I've never had anyone hint I could be some kind of femme fatale."

Josh groaned and pulled her into his arms. "What do you think these kisses have been about?" he asked as his mouth closed over hers again.

She drove him crazy. As provocative as hell and she didn't even have the slightest clue. As innocent as a babe, which enchanted him and confused him. He didn't want to feel anything for her. He wanted her gone.

But not just yet. His tongue tasted her sweetness, his chest savored the feel of her soft breasts pressed against him. His arms cherished the rounded body that so trustingly leaned into him. If he weren't careful, he'd want more from her than anyone had ever given, including Jeannie.

At the thought of his former fiancée, Josh's ardor dimmed.

He raised his head.

Molly opened her eyes and stared up at him, the

wonder clearly evident. He felt ten feet tall and wary as hell.

"Change your clothes," he said.

Releasing her, he tightened the belt on his robe and headed for the office. He wasn't about to fall for some starry-eyed romantic. He had his priorities, the ranch first and everything else a distant second.

Time he called the employment agency again and hurry them up on the replacement housekeeper.

Molly prepared breakfast in a daze. She couldn't believe Josh had kissed her this morning—twice. She didn't understand it.

She felt as if she were in over her head. She hated to disappoint him, but she'd reached the limit of her experience. She hadn't a clue how to progress. Even if he wanted to progress.

And by the way he pulled away, she doubted it.

By mid morning, Molly had a grocery list that didn't end. She could have called it in like she'd done the previous one. But she wanted some time away from the ranch, and to get to know the store better, see what other things she might wish to buy for meals.

She headed for the yard, wondering who would teach her how to drive one of the pickup trucks or if she needed anyone. Josh had said he would, but she didn't want to be confined in the cab of a truck with him. Her mind kicked into overdrive anytime she came near him. How could she concentrate on driving techniques if she wondered every second whether he'd kiss her again?

The only truck available was the big blue and white one nosed up against the barn. She crossed the yard and opened the door. The keys were in the ignition. Climbing up into the cab, she slammed the door and took stock. How hard would it be? A bit different from a car, he'd said. But everything looked the same. She adjusted the seat. Josh or Lance must have driven it last, the seat was so far back. Fiddling with the mirror, she took a deep breath and started the engine.

No one came to see who had started the truck. In fact, she hadn't seen hide nor hair of anyone since Josh passed through the house sometime after breakfast, fully dressed in his dry clothes. Which reminded her, she hadn't put that second wash load in the dryer. Slowly she reversed the truck until she stopped by the back door. Putting it into park, she dashed inside to pull the dry clothes from the dryer and pile them on top, throw the clothes in the dryer, start the last wash load.

In only moments she turned onto the highway that led to Cheyenne, pleased she had managed on her own and forgotten nothing. Her confidence soared.

By the end of the week, Molly felt much more secure in her position. She'd mastered shopping, meal planning, and even cooking. Only once during the week had she burned anything and she had hidden the evidence before the men discovered it. Though a couple of them sniffed the air suspiciously.

The house shone. She'd cleaned everything from top to bottom, including Josh's bedroom. Laundry still proved a challenge to remember to put wet clothes in the dryer, but she made it a habit to wander into the laundry room just after mealtime.

But her book had suffered. Too tired at night to do anything but fall into bed, she hadn't written anything.

Determined to get busy on the novel, she hurried through her chores Friday morning, giving the house a lick and a promise. Since everything had been cleaned in the last couple of days, there was little to do. She made a huge pot of stew, set it on the stove to simmer slowly, and wiped up after lunch.

The afternoon loomed free and she planned to take full advantage of it.

For the first time since she arrived, she wanted to go outside and discover what she could about the ranch.

Strolling to the barn, Molly avidly took in everything her eyes spotted. The few horses in the corral dozed in the early afternoon sun, one back leg bent, resting on the tip of a hoof, heads lowered, eyes closed.

The blue and white pickup she'd driven to the store was parked nose in by the gray barn. She smiled as she remembered how proud she'd felt the other day when she reached home without mishap. And the long assessing look Josh had given her when he found out she'd taken the truck and done enough shopping to last a couple of weeks.

The wide double doors of the barn stood open and the cavernous interior looked dark and mysterious compared to the bright sunshine. The scent of hay and horses mingled in the breeze. It was hushed, no voices murmured in the background. Most of the men were out on the range somewhere. Doing tallies, she remembered. Only four had been in for lunch.

She paused in the doorway to let her eyes adjust to the dimmer light. The hayloft ran the length of the barn on both sides, open in the middle. Bales of hay stacked up five high lined the walls. Loose hay drifted over the edge when the breeze gusted. The stalls were empty. The door to the tack room stood open and Molly headed for it.

Jack leaned back in a chair, rubbing saddle soap into a set of reins. He glanced up when she stepped inside.

"Hi. I'm taking a walk," Molly said brightly.

"Howdy. Set a spell. Finally wanting out of the house?"

"Yes. I've caught up on all the work that needs doing right away. I thought I'd find out more about the ranch."

"Any questions, ask away."

Molly glanced around. Jack had the only chair and she wouldn't ask him to give it up. She took a blanket from a hook on the wall and folded it on the floor, sinking down so she could watch Jack work as he talked.

A million questions bubbled up. Some from her own curiosity, others slanted to the new idea she had for her book. Jack answered them all patiently, expanding when she requested, explaining terms to her, making sense at last to some of the conversations she'd heard at dinner.

When a horse rode into the yard, Molly wondered if it might be Josh. She hadn't seen him since breakfast. He'd been one of the men out doing tallies, so he hadn't come in for lunch.

Her hands grew damp with nerves when she thought it might be him. He'd maintained his distance since that morning he'd kissed her in the laundry room.

But he hadn't had any reason to get angry with her since then.

She'd done her job well and though he watched her during mealtime, he found no fault. While she was pleased she was beginning to measure up, she lived in hope he'd kiss her one more time before she left.

Six

L ance appeared in the doorway.
"Wondered who you were talking to," he said to Jack, then smiled at Molly, one finger tipping back his hat.

"Just answering some questions the little lady had. Her first time on a ranch, you know," Jack said.

"Come with me, I'll give you some pointers," Lance invited.

Molly scrambled up and rehung the blanket. "Thank you, Jack. Hope I didn't drive you crazy with all my questions."

"No, pleasure to talk about ranching. So many people aren't interested in hearing an old man ramble on."

"You didn't ramble, and I found it all fascinating," she said with a sunny smile. Following Lance into the barn, she walked beside him as he led his horse to the rear. Fastening it in cross ties, he began to unsaddle his mount.

"Where did you go today?" she asked, taking careful note of how he did everything. The horse seemed large, but didn't bother Lance. He easily hefted the heavy saddle, dropping it on a stand nearby and turning to grin at Molly.

"Out to one of the areas where we've got a lot of cattle. We're taking a tally of how many are on that particular bit of range, checking to make sure we've lost none, or none are down and hurting. Or missing."

"Do you do that kind of thing a lot?"

"Enough to insure the well-being of the herd."

"The Rafter C seems to be a very prosperous ranch," she commented.

"Very. One of the top ranches in this part of the country. When Jase ran the place, he got written up in a journal as a rancher to watch."

"How long ago was that?"

"A few years now. Before I came here. Jase didn't want a foreman, did all that kind of work himself."

"And where was Josh?"

"At the university. When he graduated, he started working here as foreman, I guess you'd say."

"Then Jase left and Josh took over?"

"Yep. Once their sister graduated from the university, Jase took off to ride the rodeo circuit. Josh hired me a few months later."

"And the ranch continues to be very prosperous," she finished, feeling a certain vicarious pride in the work Josh did. His brother might have started things in the right direction, but it was Josh's direction now that kept the ranch prosperous.

"Very prosperous, but why do you care? Worried about your salary?" Josh's voice sounded behind her.

Molly turned, startled to find him standing so close.

She hadn't heard him come in. She saw his horse standing beyond the open doors. How much had he heard? And what interpretations did he put on her questions? Obviously the wrong ones.

"I wasn't *worried* about anything, just curious," she said, flustered.

His hat pulled low, his jeans were tight and dusty. Molly's heart fluttered and she longed to sit somewhere and stare at him until she had her fill. But ever conscious of Lance standing there and Josh's unfriendly stare, she looked away.

"Now I wonder why?" Josh glanced at Lance, back to Molly. "What are you doing out here?"

"I'm caught up on the housework and wanted to get out for some fresh air," she said pertly, her eyes meeting his, her gaze challenging.

"In the barn?" His tone disbelieving.

"Molly wanted to know more about the ranch. Jack answered some of her questions. I was going to show her around," Lance said easily, his gaze meeting Josh's, his stance loose and at ease.

Ignoring his foreman, Josh stared at Molly, his eyes narrowed. "I told you I'd answer any questions you had."

"You weren't here. Lance and Jack were."

"I'm here now."

"I don't mind, boss," Lance interjected.

"Don't you have work to do?" Josh asked, transferring his gaze to Lance.

"Just report in the findings from the tally. I can do it orally if you like."

"No, write it up. And when the others come in, write

up their tallies, too. And while you're waiting, you can unsaddle my horse."

Josh nodded toward the standing horse before stepping closer to Molly. Taking her arm in his hand, he tugged her toward the large double doors.

Lance hesitated a moment, then shrugged and smiled. "Sure thing, boss."

Josh marched Molly out into the yard. In the distance he saw two more men riding in. He kept hold of her arm and moved away from the barn toward the house.

"Don't you have dinner to fix?" he asked.

"We're having stew and it's simmering now." She tried to release her arm from his grasp, but he ignored her. She didn't like feeling like a recalcitrant child who had to be marched into the house.

"I told you to stay away from the men," Josh said in a low growl.

"I wasn't doing anything wrong, merely asking some questions."

"For your book?"

"Maybe some of the questions could provide me some background information. But the rest were because I'm curious."

"Why?" He stopped well before the back stoop.

"Why not? I have never lived on a ranch before. I want to find out more about it."

"Then ask me, as I told you."

"You didn't tell me I couldn't ask questions about the ranch. You just said stay away from your cowboys if I wanted to do research for my book. I wasn't flirting or anything."

He turned and started walking around the house until they reached the front porch. Before them the green grass waved gently in the afternoon breeze, the trees that shaded portions of the house rustled softly. The air was clean and fresh and only the faintest trace of hay and horse could be discerned.

Josh released her arm and sank down in one of the rockers that lined the wooden porch. Gingerly, Molly sat in the one next to his.

"Questions?" he said.

"Jack answered a lot I had," she replied.

"He's all right. Stay away from Lance."

"Why?"

"He watches you. He's interested in you. I don't want my foreman's mind on anything but his job."

"How feudal. He's entitled to a life aside from being your foreman."

"Not with some temporary woman more interested in writing about romance than—"

"Than?" she asked, her eyes narrowed as she suspected the ending of his thought.

"Than in doing chores around here."

"That isn't what you started to say, is it?"

He took his hat off and dropped it on the wooden floor beside his chair. Raking his fingers through his hair, he leaned against the high back of the rocker and watched her from lowered lids.

"That's what I said. Never mind what I started to say."

"I have a good imagination."

"I'm beginning to believe it."

Molly remained silent.

"Is it all made up? Your book, I mean?" he asked.

"Mostly." She glanced away, studied the cottonwoods that rustled in the breeze. The sound should be soothing; why couldn't she relax?

"Not from first-hand experience?"

"I don't have much experience," she said, her eyes now fixed on the distant horizon. Did she have to spell it out for him? Surely he noticed from her kisses.

"You were engaged."

"What does that have to do with anything?"

"I don't know. Tell me about the engagement."

She settled back in her rocker and pushed it to and fro. "I don't see how that has anything to do with my job here."

"It doesn't. Tell me about your engagement."

She flicked a glance and met his heated gaze. "There's not much to tell. My father introduced me to Marc. We dated. I thought him very romantic at first. He took me to fancy restaurants, ordered for me, we went dancing. He bought me nice gifts. It was all quite elegant. When he asked me to marry him, I thought it would be perfect, so I said yes."

"Of course, a woman likes presents, likes to be wined and dined. Did you ever give a thought to the years you two would live together? To building a life together?"

"I thought I did. I thought I was in love, now I think I was just infatuated with the first man who paid me attention. Disenchantment didn't take long. But it was discovering the deal my father had made with him that caused the actual break."

"What deal?"

She looked at him. "He had everything a woman could want. He's rich, well-established in his career, has a beautiful home, decorated by a professional. He likes to go out to dinner, dancing, parties. And the opportunity to become partner in my father's firm if he married me."

"Would that have been bad?"

She shrugged. "People want to be wanted for themselves, not for career advancement."

Josh looked out over the grass. Her experiences mirrored his own in a way. Jeannie had been about fun times, parties, clubs and spending money. She'd seen him as a continual source of those funds.

"So how do you write romance novels if you have no first-hand experience?" he asked.

"I told you, I have a good imagination."

Josh reached over and caught her hand in his, threading his fingers between hers. Molly looked at their linked hands. The heat from his hard palm swept through her like a range fire. The shimmering awareness flooded her. Her own sense of femininity grew and her body began to clamor for more attention. She drew in a shaky breath and slowly tightened her hold on his hand, her gaze slowly, reluctantly, drawn to his.

"Sometimes there's no substitution for experience," Josh murmured.

"Are you offering to be the man to give me some?" she asked narrowing her eyes.

Her heart pounded at the thought. If the simple

holding of hands almost had her climbing into his lap, what would a full attack on her senses do? She could imagine only so much. She never imagined a simple clasping of hands could so disrupt her equilibrium. So how could she imagine the myriad pleasures making love would bring?

"I can give you some. But strictly as research."

She smiled at his nonsense. "What else but research?"

"I don't want you getting the wrong idea. I have no intention of marrying you."

"Marriage? Why bring that up?"

"You were checking out the financial strength of the ranch with Lance. Trying to determine if it was worth your while?"

She pulled her hand. She no longer wanted to hold hands. Josh tightened his grip, refusing to release her.

"I wasn't trying to find out how rich you are. For heaven's sake, if I wanted a rich husband, I could have married Marc. I don't want any husband. I'm tired of men telling me what to do. I want a chance to do things on my own. See if I can make a life for myself. The last thing I want is to tie myself down with some bossy man who thinks he's God's gift to women."

"So there's no problem, then."

"What do you mean?"

"I'll provide you with the experience you need for your book, and we will both walk away at the end of your stay with no expectations on either side."

She stared at him, her heart caught in her throat. For a long moment she considered his suggestion. Could she do it? Could she allow kisses and caresses and write down the feelings to add authenticity to her writing? And then walk away when the book sold?

She didn't miss Marc at all. But Josh might prove different. It was like playing with fire. Could she do it and not get burned?

Josh watched the expressions chase across her face and almost smiled. She considered every aspect, he could tell. But he had no idea of the outcome. Would she want to explore the sizzling sensuality between them? Or opt to remain safe and chaste?

His palm burned where they touched. He longed to draw her into his lap and kiss her until neither could remember their names. His body wanted hers. His control wore thin around her and he didn't like it. Maybe a few kisses would purge his system of the need that grew stronger each day.

Tugging experimentally, Molly wasn't sure whether to be relieved or disappointed when he released her hand this time. She swallowed hard and faced him. Taking in the golden hair in disarray since his fingers had plowed through it, the sun-bronzed skin taut across high cheekbones, the firm lips that had already kissed her senseless, and the strong jaw that reminded her of his strength, she met his gray eyes.

"Could I think about it?"

"Sure." He reached for his hat and rose. Leaning over her, he caught her chin between his thumb and forefinger. "The offer stays open as long as you want to take to decide. But the offer is with me. Stay away from my men."

"I know." Her breath caught. He was so close he had only to lean over a few more inches and his mouth would touch hers, his lips could bring her the same heady delight she'd felt in the laundry room.

Parting her lips slightly to let the breath escape, Molly leaned forward just a little bit, to bring Josh even closer—

He straightened and rammed his hat on his head. "See you at dinner." Sauntering off, around the side of the house, he left her stunned and alone.

Molly sank back in the rocker in embarrassment. She'd practically offered herself to him and he'd walked away. Was it because she hadn't yet said yes to his proposition? Had he seen how much she wanted his kiss? She hoped not. Even if she did take him up on his offer, she wanted to stand up on her own feet not grow to depend on another man.

She rose and tried the front door. It was unlocked, so she entered the house and headed for her room. Changing from her boots to more comfortable tennis shoes, she headed for the kitchen. Time to make the cornbread and set the table. It was getting close to dinnertime. She'd think about his offer after dinner.

Molly had prepared the cornbread batter and begun to pour it into the pans when the phone rang. She jumped. It rang so infrequently, it startled her. She waited a moment to see if it was answered from the barn or something. When it rang again, she reached for the extension.

"Hello?"

"Hi, is Josh around?" a cheery feminine voice asked.

"Hold on." Molly's curiosity rose. What woman called him?

She opened the back door preparing to run to the barn to see if he was there when she saw him leaning against the corral fence watching one of the men working a horse in the corral.

"Josh, phone," she called.

He acknowledged her call with a wave and headed for the house.

Molly resumed her work as he picked up the receiver.

"Hello? Hi, Gillian, what's up?"

Molly carefully placed the pans in the hot oven, conscious of listening to his side of the call. He couldn't expect privacy if he were in the kitchen with her. If he had wanted to be alone he could have taken it in the office.

Why hadn't the caller used his cell phone? She knew they had cell service here from her own phone

"Damn! No, no, it's fine. I'm running late. I just got in. It'll take me a half hour or so to shower and dress. I'll be there before eight."

Molly carefully checked the stew pot, stirring gently, every cell in her body focused on Josh's conversation.

Who was Gillian, and where was he going to be by eight?

Josh replaced the phone and turned to Molly. He knew she'd heard every word. "I won't be here for dinner."

"I won't set a place," she replied, her eyes on the stew she stirred. *Where are you going? And with whom?* she screamed inside. She hoped her expression didn't give away her raging curiosity.

Or the unexplained hurt.

He was obviously going out with Gillian, whoever she was.

Her active imagination immediately envisioned a young sexy woman with long red hair, bright green eyes and a figure to die for. She would be scintillating and provocative. And enchant Josh all evening.

Hadn't he just propositioned her? All but asked her to have an affair with him? Now he was going out with some other woman?

She looked up to tell him she'd decided to decline his offer but he was already gone. Sure, he had to hurry and shower to leave in time to pick Gillian up by eight. He had no time to stand around waiting for her answer.

When the men came in for dinner, Billy asked right away where the boss was. He'd noticed there'd been no place set for Josh.

"Going out," Molly said, proud her voice sounded almost normal, that she hadn't growled out the words with all the frustration simmering inside. She sat at her usual place, extremely aware of the vacant chair beside her.

Josh came into the kitchen, dressed in casual slacks, a cream-colored shirt and sports jacket. He looked wonderful. After one quick glance, Molly looked away and refused to look at him again. The dull ache in her breast was not because he was dating another woman. She wouldn't let it be.

"Wowee, boss, you sure are duded up. Hot date?"

Billy asked, teasing.

Josh's face darkened. "A friend of mine asked me to escort her to a party," Josh said shortly.

"Have a good time, Josh," Jack said.

"Yeah, I'm going to town after dinner myself. It's Friday night and I've worked hard all week," Billy said.

"You go in when you haven't worked hard," Lance murmured.

Billy beamed a smile around the table. "Right. It's party night, right, boss?"

Molly felt Josh's gaze on her, but she kept her eyes on her plate. The stew had turned out to be delicious and she tried to be pleased about it.

But she was disappointed Josh wasn't eating it. He only saw her less than successful attempts. She wished he'd have eaten dinner here when she had such a success.

"I won't be late," Josh said.

"Does that mean tonight or tomorrow morning?" Billy asked irrepressibly, his spirits high.

"Billy." Lance's voice held a warning the younger man couldn't ignore. He shut up.

"Take it easy, Josh. And don't worry," Lance said, his eyes on Molly. "I'll take care of things here."

She looked up and met his gaze. Hearing the screen door slam shut, Molly knew Josh had gone. Lance smiled easily. And Molly felt marginally better.

"Want to go into town with me for a few drinks and dancing at a country-western bar?" Lance asked.

She nodded. She sure as shooting didn't want to stay home alone and let her imagination run riot thinking about Josh and the beautiful Gillian. Ignoring Josh's warnings to stay away from his men, and especially Lance, she smiled gratefully. "I'd like that. But I'm not sure how good I'll be at the dancing."

"Good enough, I'm sure." He winked and resumed eating.

The conversation around the table turned to the plans of the others. Almost all the cowboys were going into town. Jack and Trevor had plans for a television show about honeybees.

Jack offered to do the dishes, which Molly gratefully accepted.

Before long Lance and Molly were heading for town. Determined to enjoy herself, and make the evening pleasant for Lance, she hid the hurt Josh's date had inflicted, and set out to entertain. Lance laughed at the spots in her stories she wanted him to and asked enough questions to have her expound on everything. The ride to town flew by and before Molly realized it, they were walking into The Last Roundup.

Obviously popular by the friendly greetings called out, Lance waved and called greetings in return. He spotted some friends at a large table and in no time had Molly seated and introduced. Relieved to see the other women dressed in jeans and shirts as she was, she relaxed and soon was in the middle of the conversation.

It was a wonderful evening. The men took turns dancing with the women, not letting them sit out any sets. The women were friendly and Molly felt she could develop a strong friendship with one or two. If she were staying, that is.

When asked what she did, she mentioned she was

trying to write a romance novel. Heads turned and the questions and suggestions came fast and furiously. Everyone had a story of their most romantic moment. Some wanted to know what her story was about, others had ideas they wanted to write about one day.

At one point Molly laughed and waved her hands. "You have to slow down. I can't hear everyone at once. I wish I had paper and pencil to write down some of these ideas, they're great."

"We'll each write them down and send them to you. Where do you live?"

"The Rafter C. I'm the housekeeper there."

"Of course, she came with Lance."

"I didn't know housekeepers came so pretty. The one my dad had was old and crotchety," one cowboy called out, winking at Molly.

She smiled and basked in the warm friendliness of the group. They were supportive of her dreams and ambitions, not derogatory. They were friendly and helpful and fun to be with. It was so different from what she was used to, she wanted to stay forever.

The evening ended all too soon when the band played the last song. With promises to meet again ringing in her ears, Molly reluctantly climbed back into Lance's truck and settled down for the long drive home. She was smiling, humming the last song. The evening had been fun.

He played country music softly on the radio and conversation between them was desultory. When he turned onto the blacktop drive that led to the house, Molly turned to him.

"I had a wonderful evening, Lance. Thank you for inviting me."

"I'm glad you came. Think you can use any of the suggestions from tonight?"

She smiled, remembering. "Maybe one or two. I couldn't believe some of the comments, they were so outrageous. And yet others were so basic—like a simple bouquet of flowers or a home-cooked meal. It was interesting to see what different people found romantic."

"What do you find romantic, Molly?"

She shook her head. "Different things. Flowers are nice."

When he pulled into the yard a light shone in the kitchen but the bunkhouse sat in darkness. The night sky blazed with millions of stars, the moon a mere crescent low on the horizon. He killed the engine and sat back.

"What else, Molly?"

"I don't know. In my story I have plans for the heroine to give small gifts to the hero. He's not used to getting gifts and thinks that is pretty special."

"And do you—"

The passenger door snapped open, the overhead light flooding the cab of the truck.

"Where the hell have you been?"

Josh was blazing mad. He leaned into the cab and nailed Lance. "Do you have any idea how late it is?"

"After two," Lance replied easily, a smile playing around his lips as he leaned against his door and studied his boss.

"If you were going out, you could have told me!" Josh said to Molly, reaching in to unfasten her seat belt.

"What I want or don't want to do on my hours off is none of your business," she said, slapping his hands away and letting the belt slide free. When he reached for her arm, she slapped at him again. "Don't touch me!"

She turned to Lance, annoyed to find his amusement so blatant. "Thank you again."

"Good night, Molly. Sleep well." He trailed a finger down her cheek.

Josh stood by her door, ramrod straight, anger roiling off him in waves.

Molly avoided touching him as she walked to the house, her head held high.

He walked beside her like a guard.

"Where were the two of you?" he growled.

"Out," she replied, marching up the steps and into the kitchen. Not pausing a beat, she continued toward the stairs and her room.

"Where?"

"Not that it is any of your business—we went to The Last Roundup. Where I met a lot of nice people and had a grand time." She ended almost shouting.

He wasn't the only one to get angry. Who did he think he was? Her father?

"Not that it's any of your business. I didn't ask about your date."

"It wasn't a date. Was that what you and Lance had, a date?"

"Define date. If you pick up some woman and take her to a party, then bring her home, isn't that a date?"

"I told you to stay away from Lance!"

"What, stay home like a dutiful daughter while

you're out carousing? I think not."

He exhaled deeply.

"Is that what this is about? You're jealous of me taking Gillian to that party? She asked me to go with her several weeks ago. Long before I even met you."

She shrugged and continued toward the stairs. "I don't need any explanations. Your life is yours to lead as you wish. As is mine."

"While you work for me you'll do as you're told. Stay away from Lance and the other men on this ranch."

"Or?" She turned and glared at him.

"Or you're fired."

She held his gaze, seeing the implacable determination in it.

So mad she wanted to burst, Molly took a deep breath. She wouldn't lose her job over a man who meant nothing to her beyond friendship, yet she refused to let Josh run roughshod over her like this. It reminded her too much of her father. She was her own person and would fight to retain that.

"Who died and left you in charge?" she said between clenched teeth. "I'll see whomever I wish on my free time. Where do you come off dictating to me? Do you do that with everyone on the ranch? It's a wonder you can keep anyone."

He ran his hands through his hair and the anger seemed to dissipate. He lowered his hands and stared at her.

"You're right. I apologize. It is none of my business. You'd think I'd learn."

Dumbfounded, Molly's own anger evaporated. Was

this a trick? "What do you mean?"

He turned and walked slowly across the kitchen to close the back door.

"What you do with your life is your business. I have no right to tell you to stay away from Lance. I tried interfering before with disastrous results. I told my brother-in-law to stay away from my sister. She found that hard to forgive. I thought I'd learned a lesson from that. You can see whomever you wish, of course, as long as it doesn't interfere with your work or his." His back still turned toward her, he fiddled with the key in the door.

Knowing they never locked the place, Molly recognized a stalling tactic when she saw one.

"Go to bed, Molly," he said.

She didn't want to leave. Something blossomed in her heart as she watched him fiddle with the door, unwilling to turn and face her. And she remembered his offer on the porch.

"Aren't you going to kiss me good-night?"

He whirled, his eyes blazing.

"So you thought about my offer?"

She nodded. She wouldn't tell him she'd thought about it almost nonstop since he'd suggested it.

"And?"

"I'm still not sure." She wanted guarantees and knew there'd be none. Except when she left, she'd never see Josh again.

"Then we'll wait on any kisses until you are."

She licked her lips wishing she were brave enough to fling caution to the wind and commit.

"We'll only go as far as you want."

She nodded, her skin feeling too tight for her body. He looked at her and she almost flung herself against him to assuage the longings that rose so fiercely. She wanted to feel his kisses, to feel the length of his hard body pressed against her softer one. But she was afraid. Would her emotions get out of control? Could she play at love and then walk away unscathed?

Seven

"Go to bed," he said softly.

Still she hesitated. She wished she dare agree to his outrageous plan. Wished she didn't feel so inadequate and uncertain. Wished most of all she didn't feel this pull of attraction with this sexy cowboy. She was so fascinated by him. She didn't like it, but there it was.

"Tonight, at the country and western place, I met a lot of nice people. When I told them I was writing a romance novel, they had tons of ideas on what they considered romantic."

He watched her, his eyes steady and calm. Slowly he leaned against the back door and crossed his arms over his chest.

"And?"

"So, I thought maybe I should take a poll or something, find out what people find romantic and incorporate that in my book."

"You could, but I don't think you need to."

"Why not?" She was surprised.

"You're a woman, write what you find romantic."

"But what about what a man finds romantic?"

"I told you, I'm available for the time you're here."

"To tell me what you find romantic?"

He shrugged. "If you like. If that's all you want."

"I thought you wanted more."

"I do. But if you draw the line at words only, I'll abide by it. You have to make up your own mind, Molly. I'm not going to do it for you."

That was a switch. She couldn't imagine her dad or Marc saying that. She stared at him for another moment, knowing the next step had to come from her. And she knew what she wanted to do. Her senses clamored for him. She wanted to feel that electricity that charged through her whenever he touched her, wanted to revel in the sensations that lit her up like nothing else ever had. But she was wary of herself, and of Josh. She hesitated.

"I could poll the men here on the ranch. Just ask questions."

"No."

She tilted her chin. "Why not?"

"Too disruptive."

"I'm not disruptive. I would just ask questions and note their answers at dinner. We are already together then and they're not working."

"No."

"Give me a reason."

"I told you."

"If I spoke to them on their off time, I wouldn't disrupt their work."

"No."

She wanted to scream in frustration. "You remind me of my father. Issuing edicts with no real reason to back them up. Very well, I won't ask any of the men anything while we are on the Rafter C."

He eyed her suspiciously. "Or off."

She smiled triumphantly. "You can't control our actions when we are away from the Rafter C. Next time Lance asks me to go into town with him, I'll go and ask him questions all the way there and back."

Josh pushed away from the door and strode across the room to her. Excitement and anticipation shimmered just below the surface as Molly held her ground, watching him storm over to her at her provocative remarks. Did she want to provoke him?

"What's your game, Molly? Are you trying my patience deliberately or is it unintentional? Why are you here? You say you want to write a book and be on your way, yet you haven't sat down once as far as I can tell to do any work on it. And you flirt with my men, ask questions about the success of the ranch. What for? To test your wiles with these men? Or are you looking for a meal ticket?"

She shook her head, something dying inside her. He'd misinterpreted everything.

"No," she whispered. "I want to write a book. In the meantime, I need to make a living. I was pushing, I'm sorry."

How could she explain the urge that almost overwhelmed her to push and push until he gave? She didn't understand it herself, how could she make him understand?

"Go to bed," he repeated for the third time.

"Good night." She turned and hurried to her room before she gave in to the impulses that pounded through her. She wanted his kiss, but without the agreement he'd asked for. She wasn't ready to make the kind of decision he demanded.

Josh watched her hurry away and frowned. She hadn't a clue how disruptive she could be. She upset his equilibrium every time he came around her. What was her real reason for taking the job? For being so damned provocative?

He wanted her. More than he had wanted anyone in a long time. Yet he didn't trust her an inch. He'd thought Jeannie honest and sincere, only to discover she'd been more interested in the money the ranch brought in than in building a life with him.

Molly appeared to be different. Or was she? It didn't matter.

If she agreed to his terms, they'd explore the sensuality between them and call it quits when she left. He liked being with her. He found her wide-eyed wonder at the things on the ranch refreshing. Even her daydreaming intrigued. He should be mad she wasn't better attuned to the real world, but he found it enchanting. Not the burned meals, or wet clothes, but the way she tuned everything out and gazed off into space. Her return to reality was always amusing.

Though Saturday was technically her day off, and though she hadn't gone to bed until almost three o'clock, Molly rose to fix breakfast at the usual time. She hadn't slept well. Maybe she'd take a nap in the afternoon. In the meantime, she wanted breakfast; it didn't prove to be that much extra trouble to prepare it for everyone.

She cooked French toast and sausage, putting everything in the oven to keep warm. The men drifted in one at a time. Billy never did show up. Nor did Josh. Molly wondered where he was. Sleeping in?

The others appreciated her efforts and thanked her.

Excited to have the rest of the day to herself, she cleaned up the kitchen and headed for the office. Turning on the computer, she pulled up the last chapter she'd worked on and reread what she'd written. It seemed flat. Sighing, she began to edit, trying to get some spark that would reach out and grab her.

But she couldn't concentrate. Gazing out the window, she thought about all Josh had said, and suggested. Unbidden, Gillian's voice echoed in her mind. How friendly was Josh with Gillian? Had he made arrangements with Gillian for more dates?

Where did that leave her? He had said he'd abide by her guidelines. Could she take what he had to offer and set some limits? Like, not going to bed together? She wanted love and some commitment before going that far. Yet his kisses inflamed her, set her body spinning like nothing else ever had. She longed to ruffle his hair, trace those sleek muscles, taste him again. Have the right to touch.

And if she could capture some of the feelings that spilled through her every time he came near, she'd find the spark she missed in her book.

It was time to make a decision. Did she want to live life to its fullest, or stay safe and secure as her father had taught her?

"The words won't type themselves," Josh said, amusement lacing his voice.

She spun around, her heart beating rapidly at the mere sight of him. He looked wonderful.

"I was thinking."

"Yeah, I know." He walked into the office, his loose-legged gait like poetry in motion. His eyes never left hers. "If you want to see some of the ranch, come on. I'm riding out and you can go with me."

"Great!" Without a thought to her manuscript, she flicked off the computer and rose.

"I need to get my boots."

"Right. I'll meet you in the barn. Do you have a hat?"

She shook her head.

"I'll find you one. Hurry up."

"Did you get breakfast?" she asked as she passed him on the way to the stairs.

"Yes. Thanks for fixing it. You didn't have to, Saturday's your day off."

"Wasn't much bother. I'll be right there." She ran up the stairs, her thoughts spinning. Josh had asked her to go with him today. She'd get to spend as much time with him as she wanted, and learn more about ranching.

Excitement spilled through her like warm wine. She could hardly wait.

In only a short time the two of them rode away from the homestead and out to the open range. The grass grew high, making a swishing sound as the horses walked through. The sky spread from horizon to horizon in a clear deep blue, the distant mountains shone brilliant in the morning sun. The air was still.

"It's beautiful," Molly said breathlessly as she matched her horse's gait with Josh's.

"I've never wanted to live anywhere else," Josh acknowledged.

"Well, trust me, I've been all around and this is the prettiest place I've seen."

"Where is all around?"

"My dad is a contract consultant for the government. We've been in Washington, D.C., Virginia, Washington state and even California. Most recently Texas of course."

"You must have moved a lot."

"Yes. When I get my own place, I'm staying put forever. I hate moving all the time, trying to make new friends, to fit in with people who have backgrounds I can never match. I guess I'm glad I got to see different areas of the country, but I don't suffer from wanderlust."

"My dad bought this place before he married. It's been in our family now for over thirty-five years. Except when I attended the university, I've lived here all my life. Can't imagine what it would be like to move frequently."

"It's not fun. You're lucky." Wistfully Molly looked around. She'd love to belong to a place like this. To know it had been in her family for years and would continue for generations to come.

"How well can you ride?" Josh asked.

"I can stay on. Want to go faster?"

She grinned at him. The day seemed brighter by being with him. Only the two of them and the endless open range.

"Yes." He urged his mount into a lope and Molly kept up with him. The blood pounded through her veins, the wind blew past her face, cooling her heated skin. She felt so alive she tingled.

He drew up beneath a stand of cottonwood, near a pond. Slowing the horses, they walked quietly for a few minutes, then Josh stopped and dismounted. He handed his reins to Molly, his fingers brushing hers: "I need to check something." Walking deeper into the stand of trees, he studied the ground, the animal paths that led to the pond. He circled the pond and came back to Molly.

"Looking for something?"

"Checking the tracks to see who might be using this watering hole. Only cattle so far."

She nodded, her gaze caught with his. Her fingers felt numb holding his reins. Her heart caught in her throat. Mesmerized by his gaze, she could only look and hope he couldn't read the turmoil that raged through her.

"Molly?"

"Yes?"

"Have you decided yet?"

His low, sexy voice sent tendrils of sexual awareness shooting through to her fingers and toes.

She took a deep breath. Her whole life could be changed by a single word. Was she willing to chance it?

"Yes."

She tossed him the reins and quickly dismounted. Stepping closer, she raised a hand to his cheek.

"I've decided it would be very nice to have some actual experience to draw upon to write my book."

Being with him would definitely broaden her

horizons. She'd grab all the fun she could now, save the memories for when she moved on.

He let his breath out slowly—as if he'd been holding it.

Her fingers trembled against his cheek and he covered her hand with his, holding her against the warmth and strength of his jaw.

"I won't hurt you," he said gruffly.

She nodded, her eyes locked with his. He looked at her as if seeing her for the first time. Then a slow smile tilted the corners of his lips. "You're a pretty woman, Molly Forrester. That Marc was a fool to let you get away. Are you sure the proposed partnership is what drew him to you?"

Pleasure warmed her like the sun. She wished she could bottle the feeling to take out anytime she wanted. Smiling up at him, she knew nothing could mar the perfection of the day.

"I'm sure. But thanks for the compliment."

Slowly Josh leaned forward until his breath brushed against her cheeks. She saw the desire in his eyes and her heart raced in anticipation. Slowly her lids grew heavy and closed. She felt his touch, light as a feather at first, pressing against her as he claimed her lips in a kiss that promised so much.

He moved her hand to the back of his neck, released it and drew her against him in a tight embrace. His mouth moved against hers, teasing hers open, tracing her lips with his tongue before slipping inside the moist heat of her mouth to explore the shimmering waves of desire that jumbled in her.

Her hat fell off—she didn't notice.

Her horse stomped impatiently; she didn't hear it.

Her entire focus centered on Josh's mouth, his body, the wondrous sensations he caused. Heat suffused, hotter than the Texas summer sun. Desire raged, stronger than the most compelling hunger. Delight bubbled up and rushed through her.

She held on for dear life. Feeling like she was spinning away in a vortex of light and heat and air, she held on to him to keep herself anchored on the earth. It was glorious. The most wonderful thing ever to happen to her.

Slowly, slowly, he ended the kiss, pulled back just an inch, still holding her soft compliant body against his. Her eyes opened and she gazed into the molten steel of his. Had the earth shifted on its axis or was she the only one to feel like it had?

"That was nice," she said dreamily, knowing her cheeks must be flushed with the heat that poured through her.

"Nice?" He grinned. "Is that the best you can do? I don't think that's enough for your book. Should we practice some more? I'll kiss you, you tell me how you rate it. When you think you have enough for the book, we'll stop."

Her mind went blank.

She couldn't *rate* his kisses. She could only feel the sensations so foreign as they captured her body and held her enthralled. If he thought she could think coherently after kissing her like that, he had a better opinion of her abilities than she did.

She took a deep breath to tell him so, but the scent of horses, grass, and Josh's own masculinity threw her. She nodded and closed her eyes, opening her lips slightly for his next kiss. She would try to define exactly how she felt—

All good and well to plan to be analytical when being kissed. Until his mouth moved over hers, until his hands rubbed her back, moved around her ribs to cup the weight of her breasts and send shooting spirals of pure hunger deep in her body. She could not think, could not analyze, only feel. And the feelings were miraculous, amazing, truly amazing.

They were both breathing hard when he ended the kiss. "Well?"

"*Very nice.*"

He groaned and rested his forehead against hers. "What do I have to do to get beyond nice?"

She giggled softly and rubbed her nose against his. "I think it's me. I think you've fried my brains and I'm stuck on that word. Really, the kisses are better than nice. I've never been kissed so—nicely—in my life."

"When we get back to the house, I'm going to see if we have a thesaurus for you."

"You didn't think they were nice?" she asked in mock shock.

"No, I thought they were the knock-your-socks-off kind of kisses that have me wanting to rip this shirt off your body so I can feel your silky skin. I want to taste every inch of you, feel the weight of your breasts in my hands. See if my mouth on other parts of your body will drive me as wild as kissing your lips does."

She swallowed. The image he painted in her mind sprang up as clear as if he'd already done it. But everything moved too fast for her. For a second she was strongly tempted to give in, but knew she needed to keep some perspective.

Clearing her throat, she pulled back a little, as much as his strong arms would allow.

"Maybe we should slow down a bit," she said, searching his eyes. She didn't want to disappoint him, but there was only so much she could take. She didn't want to do everything today.

"This is slow," he said.

"Not for me."

Sighing, he released her and reached over to get her hat. Gently he placed it on her head. "You're the boss. We'll go at whatever speed you want. But you have no one but yourself to blame if I become impatient. Kissing you is like setting fire to gasoline. I want to explode."

She beamed at him. "Josh, you say the most marvelous things. I can use them in the book!"

He frowned. "I'm not saying them to have you write them in some book."

"I thought this whole reason for doing this was to help me with my book."

Did he mean that? Was he speaking directly to her as a woman? Molly didn't want to let the thought gain a foothold. She'd set herself up for heartbreak if she did.

He brushed his thumb across her damp lips.

"The idea is to give you some first-hand experience so your writing can be more realistic. But it's also to have a bit of fun along the way—for both you and me."

"Right." Her smile came from the heart. "I'm having fun."

"Sure, with *nice* kisses."

"Very nice kisses. I'll try to come up with other adjectives, if that would make you feel better."

"All men like knowing their kisses are *nice*. Of course, I'll have to work on my technique. I would like a wonderful or exciting sometime."

"They were wonderful."

"No changing things now. You said they were nice. I'll have to work harder, that's all."

The glow from their banter warmed her heart. Josh's sense of fun surprised her. In addition to being the sexiest man she'd ever known, he could laugh at her and have her laugh with him. Did he have any idea what he did to her when he drew near? His teasing delighted her, and made her wish they could be friends forever. She wouldn't change things. If her book didn't sell right away, maybe she could stay a bit longer at the Rafter C.

He pulled her hat down on her forehead. "Come on, Molly, time to ride."

By the time they returned home, the sun sat low on the horizon. Josh had shown her the cattle and the calves. He'd explained roundups and branding, and how he culled the steers for market.

Molly had asked endless questions. While she wanted to learn every aspect of ranching, she also adored listening to his voice. She watched him talk, watched the love of his ranch shine through in his every word. And she basked in his attention.

"Thank you," she said as they reached the barn. "I had a wonderful day."

"Good. Go on inside and get cleaned up. I'll take care of your horse."

"I'll fix supper," she suggested, dismounting gingerly. Her legs felt like cooked spaghetti. Surreptitiously she clung to the saddle hoping Josh wouldn't notice. She bet Gillian rode hours every day and had no trouble once she dismounted.

She frowned. She didn't want to think about his girlfriend after the day they'd spent together. Not after the kisses they'd shared. Not after the agreement they'd struck.

He took the reins and nodded. "Something light. The men will have already eaten."

"Soup and sandwiches?" she suggested, testing her knees. She thought they would hold her.

"Peanut butter again?"

Raising her nose in the air, she let go of the saddle and headed for the house, turning at the last minute and giving him a disdainful look. "I make wonderful peanut butter sandwiches, you should be so lucky to have me make you some."

He chuckled and headed for the barn.

Molly waited until he entered before turning back toward the house. She'd take a quick shower and then fix them something. Only the two of them, it would be a nice dinner. Grimacing at the adjective she vowed she would come up with a whole vocabulary of spectacular ones to use in the future. She felt more than *nice* about the whole situation.

By the time she showered and donned fresh clothes, Molly acknowledged that she was so tired she could scarcely see straight. The lack of sleep the night before combined with all the time spent in the fresh air and sunshine riding made her wonder if she could stay awake long enough to eat dinner.

She didn't want to miss any time with Josh, not after embarking on their experiment. And after dinner she might just take him up on that offer to find a thesaurus.

Molly thought to have a quiet dinner *à deux*, but she'd underestimated the draw of someone else's cooking to the cowboys. While they'd all grabbed something to eat, Jack came to the kitchen for coffee, Billy came by to see if there was anything for dessert. Trevor and Pete wandered in to see what kept the other two and sat at the table enjoying a cup of coffee.

Giving up trying to get Josh to herself, Molly finished her dinner, put her plate in the dishwasher and wandered down to the office.

If Josh wanted to talk with his men, she'd work on her book. Flicking on her computer, she sat down with the best of intentions. But as she stared blankly at the words on the screen, she knew she wouldn't get anything done tonight. She was too tired to see straight, much less be creative.

It was comfortable in the old house. In the background she heard the rumble of the men's voices. Outside the wind blew gently, rustling the leaves of the trees. The clock on the wall by the door ticked softly. Maybe she'd close her eyes for just a second. If she didn't feel more awake soon, she'd give up and go to bed.

"Molly?" Josh shook her gently.

Slowly she lifted her lids and gazed at him. "What?" Blinking as she tried to wake up, Molly glanced around. She was still in the office.

"Go to bed, Molly. You're asleep at your desk," he said softly.

"I'll never get this book written at this rate," she complained.

"You can do some more work tomorrow. It's Sunday. Take the whole day to work on your book. No meals for anyone but yourself."

She smiled. She wanted her hero to be just like Josh, with his sexy voice, his killer smile and his gentle touch and his concern for the heroine.

"Come on, Molly." He scooped her up from the chair and carried her from the room.

"I could walk," she said, encircling his neck with her arms and resting her head against his shoulder. Closing her eyes, she relished the sensation of being carried. No one had ever done that for her before.

"Aren't I heavy?"

"Yeah, you weigh a ton," he said, chuckling.

She pulled back at that. "Put me down!"

"So you can fall asleep on your feet?" he asked, beginning to climb the stairs.

"I didn't sleep very well last night." She gave up her token struggle and rested her head against his, closing her eyes, burrowing into the warmth of his shoulder.

"And we had a full day today."

"Mmm." Full and wonderful.

He pushed open her door and crossed the room to lay her on the bed. Molly kept her eyes closed while Josh pulled off her shoes and pulled a comforter over her.

"See you in the morning," he said.

She smiled, turned to her side and promptly fell back asleep.

Josh stared down at her for a long moment, struck by the trusting way she slept.

He thought back to Jeannie and how she had calculated every move. At the time he'd thought her carefree and fun, but in retrospect he saw how she had manipulated things to go exactly the way she wanted.

If he hadn't found her in the arms of that other man, he might have gone through with the wedding.

If he hadn't heard her admit money was more important than anything, he might have been tempted to listen to her when she tried to explain the passionate embrace he interrupted.

Was Molly capable of such manipulation?

He hadn't seen anything to suggest it, but she was a woman. It would be a long time before he trusted someone with his heart, if ever. And when the time came, he wanted a woman he could depend on. Someone more like his mother than this flighty daydreaming woman. His mother hadn't forgotten to dry clothes, she hadn't burned meals, or prepared insubstantial amounts. And she sure hadn't gone off into another world when she had work to do.

He hoped Molly'd get started on her book tomorrow. The sooner she finished it and left, the sooner life would settle down again.

Josh left the room without a backward look. The desire he felt around her didn't diminish. Her kisses were a curious mix of innocence and sensual provocation. Her wide-eyed wonder at the love play between them made him feel like some sort of superhero, yet he knew where that could lead, if he believed it.

She was here temporarily, and he was willing to play while she stayed. But it would end when she left. He wouldn't think that far ahead, but take one day at a time.

Eight

Molly woke late the next morning. Knowing it was her one remaining free day for the week, she took her time getting dressed, donning a denim skirt and a pink scooped-neck shirt. She wore sandals instead of her usual tennis shoes. She didn't plan to go out to the barn and if she wanted to take a walk later, she'd go on the paved driveway.

By the time she ventured downstairs it was drawing close to noon. The house sounded empty. She fixed herself some toast and tea, ate, then wandered around the first floor looking for Josh. He wasn't around. Not that she cared.

She wondered where he had gone. Did he take a day off? Was he out on the range or in the barn? Didn't matter. She wasn't going to seek him out.

Wandering into the office, she opened the window to enjoy the fresh air while she worked. On her desk lay a thesaurus. She sat down and drew it toward her with a smile on her face. A bookmark stuck up between the pages and she turned to find the word *nice* underlined. She smiled slowly when she saw the bold handwritten notes in the margin. *See stupendous, mind-boggling, glorious, fantastic, phenomenal, extraordinary.* Stunned, she stared at the bold handwriting. Was that the way he saw her kisses, or thought she should see his?

He was right, his kisses had been fantastic. Gazing out the window, she could clearly remember every second of each kiss they'd shared beneath the trees yesterday. Heart-pumping, toe-tingling kisses unlike any she had ever experienced. Her body tingled in response twenty-four hours later. The gentle breeze stirring cooled her heated cheeks. Her eyes closed as she relived their ride. Sighing softly, she opened them. Enough time spent on memories. She had work to do.

She began to type. Could she express on paper the kind of emotions she felt? Express so the world would understand the feelings that clamored for more of his touch, more kisses?

Could words she used capture the beauty of the day, how the sun had warmed the air and ground, how the breeze had skimmed across her cheeks, cooling the heat his touch raised?

Could she put down in black and white the feelings that threatened to overwhelm her when he drew her into his embrace or when his warm gray eyes threatened to swamp her good sense with the desire so evident she could see it with her own eyes closed?

She wanted to. But how could she put into words the wonder that had engulfed her? Staring out the window, her mind saw them together in the shade of the big cottonwoods, Josh's hands tracing patterns of delight against her back, his mouth demanding a response from hers that she had never before given.

The clock chimed softly. Molly glanced its way, then back to the screen. She'd been there over an hour and not completed a single paragraph. Sighing, she began to type once again, trying to infuse her story with the delights she'd experienced.

At the back of her mind hovered the constant curiosity of where Josh had gone. From the conversation she heard in the kitchen last night, the men weren't working today. Had Josh ridden out to check something?

Or, the unbidden thought crept in, had he gone to see Gillian?

Restless she took a break and went to the kitchen for a glass of water. As she drank, she noticed the blue and white truck was gone from its usual spot by the barn. Josh must have taken it.

Sighing softly, she put the glass on the counter and wandered out onto the front porch. She wished she knew if he'd gone into town to see that Gillian. How long had he known her? Was she pretty? Was she waiting patiently for Josh to get over his former fiancée's betrayal, ready to step right up when he wanted to love again?

And why not? He had a perfect right to see whomever he wished. He had made no commitment to her. And Molly wasn't staying for long.

Yet she found it hard to hold on to the thought. She didn't like thinking that his wild kisses meant nothing. Though he'd been up-front with her that their affair would be of short duration, lasting only as long as she remained on the ranch, he hadn't said anything about seeing her exclusively.

It was peaceful on the porch. She sat back in a rocker, pushing it back and forth. Occasionally she heard a muffled thump when one of the horses in the corral kicked away a fly.

She could see for miles, endless stretches of green pasture, with the silhouette of the mountaintops to the west.

The steady motion of the rocker soothed jangled nerves. Slowly her mind began another exploration of her feelings around Josh Hart. She remained lost in daydreams for a long time.

Josh turned onto the driveway for the Rafter C in a bad mood. It was getting late and he'd spent the day in Texarkana, visiting his sister and her new husband, Jake. He'd left to get away from Molly, to give her the day free to write on her book. And to give them some time apart.

While physically he might desire her, he didn't want her getting the wrong idea about a relationship between them. It was strictly a short-term affair.

But he hadn't counted on thinking about her all day long. The drive over had been bad enough, though he had played the radio loudly trying to drown out her image that popped up tirelessly. But when Brianna cross-examined him on the new housekeeper, he found himself thinking of Molly even more. Fortunately, Jake had headed his wife off from her relentless questioning and for part of the afternoon Josh had put thoughts of Molly aside. Until he headed for home.

When he'd thought of Molly during the day he'd

envisioned her working on her book, glad he'd taken off to leave her the time to work spending the entire day at her computer.

He pulled up into the yard near a group of his men leaning on the corral fence, watching as Billy did some trick riding. The stock horses had been moved from the corral, only Billy and his gelding remained, showing off. Molly stood in the midst of the men, laughing at Billy's antics. And right next to her stood Lance McCord.

At the sound of the truck, Molly turned. Seeing Josh drive in, her heart kicked. She smiled and waved, then turned back to watch Billy lest someone guess how glad she was that Josh was home.

Her heart beat faster as she threw a smile toward Lance. She didn't want Josh to suspect how much she missed him. Yet the air seemed clearer, the smell of dust and horse and hay stronger. Every sensation sharpened. She heard the door slam behind him and in only seconds he'd joined her by the rail.

"Get much writing done?" he asked laconically, glancing at Lance.

Lance looked over, his eyes narrowed, while Molly nodded.

"A bit."

"Thought you'd still be at your computer," Josh continued.

"Nope, finished for now. I'm taking a break."

His eyes traveled down the length of her, taking in her bare arms and the low neck of her shirt, her short skirt, her long tanned legs, the ridiculous sandals she wore, the pink polish on her toenails.

"Not dressed for hanging around a corral," he said, his eyes resting on the tempting expanse of her fair skin just above her neckline.

"I think she looks great," Lance said, smiling at Molly, shifting slightly to close the distance between them.

Josh's head jerked up and he glared at his foreman. "Her feet are already dirty from the dust."

Molly looked up at him, then down at her dusty feet. Josh was right, but so what. They were her feet. So she'd have to wash them, big deal.

She turned back to watch Billy, aware of the tension radiating from Josh. She had hoped he would like to see her in a skirt. She'd worn jeans since she arrived.

"They'll wash. I think she looks great," Lance said, reaching out to smooth a lock of Molly's hair around one finger, rubbing it with his thumb.

Josh knocked his hand away, yanking her hair.

"Ow!" Molly turned to glare at him.

The men turned their attention to Josh and Lance, forgetting Billy temporarily. Two of them shuffled back and leaned against the fence. This might prove more entertaining than Billy and his horse.

"Don't you have something else to do?" Josh asked Lance in a dangerously low voice.

Lance smiled and shook his head. "Nope. This is Sunday, my day off. I'm just enjoying myself."

Josh glanced around at the faces of the other men. They were attuned to the scene playing out before them and one or two looked confused.

"Come with me." Josh wrapped his hand around

Molly's bare arm and headed for the house.

"What's up?" she asked, skipping a step trying to keep up. "Is something wrong?"

Besides her own heart rate that threatened to race out of control. The shimmering waves of sensation that shot through her from his touch were exciting.

"I thought you were going to write today. I left you alone all day so you'd have plenty of time for writing and what do I find when I get back but you're out there flirting with every man on the place."

She set her feet and jerked them to a stop, wincing as his hand tightened on her arm.

"Wait a minute, Josh Hart. I wasn't flirting with anyone! I simply took a break and came outside. I've written over a dozen pages today, a good output from me. But I got blurry-eyed at the computer and when I went outside for a walk, Billy sat there bragging about some kind of tricks he could do on his horse. So I went to watch. Just because the others watched, too, hardly counts as flirting!"

"What about the way you're dressed?"

"What's wrong with the way I'm dressed?" She glanced down. The pink shirt looked clean, despite leaning against the corral rail. The blue denim skirt had creased across her lap from sitting all day, but there was nothing wrong with it.

"These men work hard all week and on the weekend are ready to let loose. A couple of them have girlfriends, but the rest play the field. And, honey, you look ready to play."

His forefingers traced the neckline of her shirt,

skimming across the soft swells of her breasts like a hot brand.

She slapped his hand away and looked furtively toward the corral. The men were still watching them. Lance's smile could be seen from where she stood.

She looked at Josh, unsure what he was up to.

"I can dress the way I want."

She shook off his hold on her arm and turned to the house, her head held high. The man had a screw loose, there was no other explanation. She wasn't flirting, wasn't doing anything she shouldn't.

She could be packed and gone within the hour. She refused to consider where she would go so late on a Sunday night. He still owed her a week's pay, that would be enough to get a motel room somewhere. First thing tomorrow, she'd have to find another job.

She pulled her empty suitcases from beneath her bed and began to load her clothes in them.

"What are you doing?" Josh stood in the open door. She hadn't heard him follow her.

She glanced over, resumed unloading the dresser drawer. "It should be obvious, I'm packing."

She threw another stack of shirts in.

"You know, Josh, you never did finish telling me why the other housekeepers left. Did you drive them away too? Were they talking with cowboys and you accused them of flirting? Do you even know what flirting is?"

"I do know and you look as provocative as hell standing around a group of horny men," he roared.

Her eyes widened and she stared at him in astonishment. He found her provocative? In a denim skirt and cotton shirt?

"Are you crazy?" she whispered, stunned at the thought.

"Maybe." He took a step into her room, his eyes never moving from hers. "It's bad enough during the week when you wear those snug jeans that display every inch of your rounded bottom and long legs. Do you know how many times I've wanted to reach out and touch you, jeans and all? Now you have a short skirt that shows almost every inch of those long legs of yours. Your skin looks as soft as rose petals. Do you have any idea how much I want to touch you?"

She noticed his hands were clenched into fists. To keep from reaching out to her? She caught her breath, her heart slamming against her ribs. Her skin tingled all over. She opened her mouth, but he spoke before she could say a word.

"What would the bare skin of your arms feel like wrapped around my neck? You've hugged me before, but always wearing shirts with sleeves. And that neckline is too low. I can see the beginning swells of your breasts, the hint of a shadow between them."

His eyes locked with hers and Molly saw the burning heat.

She swallowed hard, trying to escape his gaze, unable to move a muscle.

"And the top is too loose. Remember how I held you yesterday beneath the cottonwoods? I remember every inch of your delectable body, and I could so easily slip my hands up beneath that top and trace every inch of you. You don't find that provocative?"

As if in a daze, Molly slowly took a step closer. Her gaze held his. Her heart raced, the blood pounding through her veins. No one had ever waxed so poetic about her before. Never.

Molly halted mere inches from him, her head tipped back to maintain eye contact. Josh groaned softly and reached for her. He pulled her against him and just held her, his head dropping to find her mouth, claim her lips with his own. Sealing them both in a world of touch and feel and exploding sensations.

Her bare arms wrapped around his neck as Molly opened her mouth and welcomed him.

His hand roamed over her back, down to cup the curve of her bottom, lifting her slightly against him, snuggling her close. Then one hand slipped beneath the loose top, tracing the long line of her spine, dipping beneath the waistband of her skirt, back up to find and unfasten her bra. Slowly, Josh eased her away enough to bring his hand around her ribs, slowly, ever so slowly, up to cup the weight of her breast.

She sighed into his mouth and pressed against him. The fiery conflagration he built threatened to overwhelm her, to sweep her away. She wanted to smile at the delight that pierced her, but she dare not release his mouth for a second. It was heaven on earth and she wanted to savor every bit of it.

When his thumb brushed across her nipple she whimpered and arched into him, seeking more attention, seeking more of him.

Josh broke the kiss to trail a string across her cheek, along her jaw, down to the pounding pulse point at the base of her throat. He brushed his thumb against her again as Molly became almost frantic. She arched her body against his as if trying to bury herself in him, whimpering in frantic demanding need.

"Shh," Josh whispered, moving to nip her earlobe, soothe it with his tongue. "Easy, baby, easy. Slow down." He slid his hand around to her back, rubbing her as he would gentle a fractious horse.

Molly clung to him, to keep from falling, her cheek against his, her arms tight around his neck. She clenched her eyes tightly and tried to get her breathing under control, tried to stop the roiling sensations that racked her. She knew he wanted her. He had told her more than once. Why had he stopped?

His hands were like hot brands on the bare skin of her back. She burned from the heat they generated. She hated to part from him, but nothing had changed. Perplexed, she wondered why he'd kissed her.

"Are you all right?" he asked softly.

She nodded. "But I don't think I know what's going on," she said against his ear. She kissed his cheek then drew back so she could see into his eyes.

"Nothing's going on. We're moving too fast, is all."

He ran one hand through his hair, and moved across to the window.

Molly watched him, hoping he would say something to change things. Afraid he never would. She eyed her suitcases. Should she pack or not?

She stared at him a long time. "It's because of Jeannie, isn't it? You're objecting to the way I am because of her. Something about me reminds you of her."

He remained quiet for so long, she didn't think he'd respond. Then he sighed and nodded. "She's the reason I want you to stay away from the men. Especially dressed like that."

"Jeannie dressed provocatively," Molly guessed shrewdly.

He nodded. "That and more."

"More?"

He nodded and lean against the sill. "I told you Jeannie wanted the money from the ranch, not the owner."

"Yes." She watched him warily. A hint of trepidation crept in.

"But I didn't tell you how I found out."

She shook her head. He gazed out over the range. Or was he looking back several years?

"I came home early one day from a cattle sale, thinking to celebrate the sale with Jeannie. She'd been staying for the week. I came upstairs and found her in bed with one of my ranch hands."

"Oh, God." Shocked, Molly didn't know what to say.

"I heard them as I climbed the stairs. So I made sure I didn't make any noise once I suspected what was going on. They'd left the door open."

Josh fell silent for a moment. "She didn't expect me home that day."

Molly stepped closer. She wanted to reach out and touch him, offer some kind of comfort but she didn't know if he'd want it or not. He looked completely self-sufficient standing at the window. Matter of fact in his telling of the scenario.

"They were laughing and talking about how she would have lots of money once she married me and if they were discreet they could continue to see each other. I think she was completely floored when I appeared in the doorway and spoke."

Molly reached out and covered one clenched fist with her own hand. She wished she could do something to ease his pain.

"I'm sorry," she said.

"Yeah, I was, too." He took a deep breath and turned to look at her. "Not only did I lose my fiancée, but one of the best hands that worked here. And made two others so upset they left, as well. I won't put up with the same kind of disruption that caused. I have asked you and told you to stay away from the men. Do you understand why?"

She nodded. "Not only do I understand, I understand with your reasoning. Why not explain at the beginning?"

"It really wasn't any of your business," he said.

Molly felt as if she'd been slapped. She released her hold on his hand and stepped back.

"Of course, you're right. It wasn't then and it isn't now. Thank you, however, for explaining. Once I have an explanation, I can comply with rules and regulations. It's the arbitrary and capricious ones I can't handle."

"Molly, I—"

"No, you're well within your rights as boss to request I stay away from the other employees on the ranch except as my job dictates. I'll make sure I don't overstep again." She wanted him gone. Her heart ached for his unhappy experience, but she was not Jeannie and if he couldn't tell the difference, she felt sorry for him."

"You'll stay?"

She nodded. She had nowhere else to go. She had no other job lined up. No place to stay unless she wanted to crash at Bethany's again.

Maybe this was a warning to make contingent plans. She was at the total mercy of this man. If he fired her she had nowhere else to go. Not a good position to be in.

"Okay, then."

He crossed her room. Molly waited until she heard his boots on the stairs before following him to close her door. It was her day off and she had no responsibilities around the ranch. She'd sneak down later and get something to eat, but for as long as she could, she would avoid Josh Hart.

She unpacked, his cold words echoing in her mind. *It was none of your business.* True. Why did it hurt so much?

Had she expected more because of his kisses? He had offered to give her some sexual experience to aid in the writing of her book. He was attracted to her, as she was to him. Sexual attraction. It meant nothing more to him, obviously. And it would mean nothing more to her!

Brushing off her dusty feet, she lay down on her bed and stared at the ceiling and thought about all Josh had told her.

Molly made him so mad sometimes he wanted to shake her! He was jealous, pure and simple. And he hated it!

He stormed into the office and yanked out his chair. Plopping down in it, he glared at her computer, the terminal still blinking. She'd drive a saint crazy. And as his sister could attest, he was no saint.

He tilted back in the chair and glanced up toward the ceiling. She tied him in knots and he didn't like it one bit. She was just a temporary housekeeper, and not a very good one at that. Maybe she should leave.

She had enough experience with kisses now to write a book on that alone. And if he didn't cool things down, he could push her farther than she wanted to go, as in all the way, with naked bodies tumbling in bed, and hot kisses everywhere.

As the minutes ticked by and it remained silent upstairs, Josh grew impatient. Maybe he'd come on a bit strong, but the image of Jeannie and Walt Hamilton wouldn't go away. Josh had seen Lance's attitude around Molly. He didn't want Lance and Molly involved. If it came to that, he'd have to let them both go. And Lance was too good a foreman to lose.

Would she stay away from Lance now that she knew the reason he'd requested it?

Would she stay away from him?

Where was she? He rose and walked into the hall. Glancing up the stairs, he saw the closed door. For a moment he considered going up and demanding she open it so he could see her again. But he didn't. Something told him he'd done enough damage for one day.

Turning back to the office he crossed to her computer. If she'd finished for the day, he should shut it off. But he hesitated, drawn to the words displayed on the screen. Slowly he sat before the monitor and read the sentences. Pressing the arrow key, he moved back to the beginning and began to read.

He shook his head. He'd never read a romance novel, but he had read plenty of fiction. He didn't think the quality demands for writing for romance would be any less.

But her writing wasn't very good. The characters were stick figures. There was no emotion. The movements were artificial.

And it broke his heart.

She wanted to write so much, had such glowing plans for when she became published. She was revolving her entire life on the hope of making it big as a writer. If this was a sample, he knew she had a long way to go.

When he got to the passage where the hero kisses the heroine for the first time, he slowed down, reread it. It showed promise. At least she didn't call it *nice*. Maybe her lack of experience did hold her back. He wondered if the couple in the book would have a fight, like they'd had a few minutes ago. How would they react, would they make up or stay mad?

He was curious as to how she planned to handle the story, and if she could make it come alive. When he reached the end, he saved everything in case she had not yet done so and turned off the computer.

Sitting at the chair she used, gazing out the open window, he wondered if the fact the hero resembled him was coincidence or not. She'd started the book before she arrived at the Rafter C, but the man sure sounded like him.

Or a nicer Josh, more how a woman might want a man. Was she using him for more than just a means to garner experience? Was she patterning everything for the hero on his life? How long would it take her to finish the book, mail it off and learn its fate? How long was she staying?

It was dark by the time Molly crept down the stairs. She didn't see Josh as she went into the kitchen to fix herself a sandwich. Pouring a large glass of ice tea, she took her makeshift meal and headed back to her room. At the bottom of the steps his voice stopped her.

"Come eat out on the porch, Molly. The evening's warm and there's no wind tonight."

She hesitated. It would be safer in her room. Did she want to beard the lion once more before the day ended?

"Molly?" The voice beguiled, entreated.

Or was it her imagination? He sounded as he always did.

"Okay." She turned and went out onto the porch. Josh held the door for her. "Did you eat?" she asked as she sat down carefully in a rocker.

"A while ago. I got a sandwich, too. My sister fixed a big meal at lunch."

"That's where you were today?"

So he hadn't been with Gillian. For no reason at all, she felt a small weight lift from her shoulders.

"I went into Texarkana to see her and her new husband."

"The man you told to stay away from her," Molly clarified.

"Yeah. Only that was before they were married. Obviously he didn't listen to me."

"Are they happy?"

"Very. An afternoon around them is all I can take," Josh said wryly.

He didn't begrudge his sister her happiness. He just no longer expected the same thing for himself.

She nibbled on her sandwich knowing he had once thought to be happily married by now to Jeannie. No wonder he didn't want to be around his sister. It must hurt.

She felt it sometimes herself. She'd once thought she'd be married by now. While she sometimes envied other people their happiness, she tried to remain patient. Someday love might come. And if not, at least she had her writing.

"And your brother's married, too, isn't he?" she asked as the silence grew.

"Yes. To a little bit of a woman who has him wrapped completely around her little finger. He's crazy about her. Even gave up the rodeo circuit for her once they were married. Though not until he won a belt buckle he's extraordinarily proud of."

"That's nice." Molly smiled. She wished she could find a man to wrap around her little finger. Someone who would want to please her all the time.

"Jase seems to like it."

"But you wouldn't?"

"Probably not."

"Do they visit the ranch a lot? Didn't you say you all own it jointly?"

"We do. Jase and Shannon come by in the fall. If they attend some of the home football games at the university, they'll come over and stay the rest of the weekend here. Brianna comes most summers for a few weeks. I don't know her plans for this summer. She and Jake just got married a couple of months ago."

"Even though they have ownership interest, you really run the place, don't you?"

"Are you interested in me as a man, Molly, or as the hero for your book?" he asked suddenly.

She almost choked on a bit of tuna. "My book?" Dread and alarm reared up.

"I read it while you were upstairs."

"You read my book?" She threw the rest of the sandwich on the plate. "You had no business reading my manuscript. It's a long way from finished and I don't want anyone reading it until it is."

"Too late, I read it. I'm not sure I like the hero."

Nine

"Isn't that why you're writing it, for others to read?" Josh asked.

"Not before it's finished. There's a lot of work to be done on it. This is just a first draft."

He shrugged. "You left the computer on. I read the display."

"Next time exercise a little control and stay away from my computer!" Molly bit her lip, unsure if she wanted to know more.

"How did you like it?" she asked, at last. Her first critic. She held her breath waiting for him to reply.

Josh hesitated.

"It's awful, isn't it?" she moaned. Darn, she knew it wasn't ready to submit, but was it so bad he couldn't find anything positive to say?

"It's a bit wooden. As if you don't know how to describe the characters so they show depth. And the scene where he kisses her is bland."

"I just haven't reached my stride yet," she mumbled, disappointed he hadn't liked what she'd done so far. "And it's only a first draft."

"Come on." Josh stood up and held open the screen

door.

"Where?" Molly rose and entered the house. His hand at the small of her back guided her down the hall to the office.

Josh snapped on the light and led her to her computer. Taking the plate from her, he put it on his desk. Pressing on her shoulders, he sat her in the chair, reaching across her to flip on her computer.

"Bring up the kiss scene," he said, drawing another chair closer and sitting beside her.

Her face warm with heat, Molly complied, her eyes scanning the words. Bland and boring and not at all like what she wanted to portray. Not at all like the pictures in her head. Why couldn't she get it right?

"Now, look this way," he said.

She turned obediently.

Josh smiled at her and cupped her chin. Lightly brushing his lips across hers, he pulled back and looked at her.

"How was that?"

"Fine."

"No, how do you feel?"

Her heart pounded as if she had run a race, her chin tingled from his touch, her eyes were dazzled by the sight of him. She used all her willpower to keep her hands gripping the arms of the chair. She wanted to reach out for him, hold him tightly against her and drown in his kisses.

"Breathless?" she asked.

He cocked an eyebrow and smiled. "Write that down."

"What?"

"Write down the kiss and what you feel."

He released her chin and sat back, watching her.

Conscious of his gaze, Molly turned to the computer and tried to capture the feelings of that brief touch of his lips against hers and the riot of sensations it caused. Her fingers felt clumsy. She kept hitting the wrong keys, but gradually she tapped out the words that closely mirrored how she felt from his kiss.

"Next one," Josh said.

"Next one what?" She turned to look over her shoulder.

"Next kiss." He turned her to face him and lowered his mouth to hers. Gently moving against her lips, he teased her, drawing his tongue along the seam, nipping gently at her lower lip when she opened to him. All too soon he sat back, a satisfied expression gleaming in his eyes.

"Write how you feel."

Molly stared at the screen unable to think. Slowly her fingers began to type the words that tried to express the heat that simmered in her veins, the yearning for more that filled her being; the delightful awareness, the increased sensitivity being with Josh generated.

Finally the words came to a halt.

"Next one."

She took a deep breath. Anticipation bubbled through her like fine wine. How many more kisses would there be? If each got more erotic, she'd be so dazed she wouldn't be able to type. Eagerly she swiveled her chair and gazed up at him.

"Next one," she confirmed.

He studied her for a long moment. The heat in his eyes ignited her. She watched as his hands came up to slowly thread through her silky hair. When he tilted her head back and took in the length of her neck, her jawline, the answering fire in her eyes, Molly grew impatient. She wanted more. Slowly Josh drew her even closer for his kiss. His breath mingled with hers as he held his lips scant millimeters from hers.

"Josh," she entreated.

"Anticipation adds spice," he murmured, touching his tongue to the corner of her mouth.

Molly tried to lean closer, but his hands held her exactly where he wanted her.

"Not yet."

"Yes," she whispered, her hands coming up to clasp around his wrist, tugging him closer.

"You always smell like roses. Is it your hair, or your body, or the essence of you?" he asked, skimming hot kisses along her jaw.

She moaned softly and closed her eyes to better savor the exquisite delights that sparkled through her.

"Are you taking note of every feeling so you can put it in your book?" he asked as his lips touched hers.

Before she could reply, he deepened the kiss, opening her mouth and searching the warmth he found with his tongue.

Molly lost track of time and place and self, absorbed by the fiery heat that built from his mouth to hers. Her body ached for his touch. His hands gently kneading her scalp weren't enough. She wanted to feel him against her, revel in the pleasure her body took from his. To know the differences between them that his hard frame suggested when pressed against her softer one.

"Write about that," he said, breathing erratically.

Molly shook her head, but it did nothing to clear the spinning sensation. She glanced at the computer screen, then back at Josh. Half rising, she moved from her chair to his lap and encircled his neck with her arms.

"You're kidding, right?" she said, trailing kisses along his cheek, feeling the rough abrasion of his day-old whiskers.

"I could no more type a word than I could ride a bronc right now."

Her mouth moved to his and she delighted when he pulled her tightly against his chest and resumed their kiss.

He kissed her neck, licking the pulse point at its base. Moving one hand to the front, he slowly began to unfasten her buttons.

One hand threaded through his thick hair while the other mimicked his as she began to release the buttons on his shirt.

His mouth claimed hers again and again. When Molly felt the cool night air on her skin, she knew she was losing her shirt. Josh moved to unfasten her bra.

"No."

She sat up and held her hand across her breasts. Blinking in the light, she stared at him, uncertainty evident in her eyes. His shirt hung halfway off his shoulder, opened to the waist. His bronzed skin shone in the lamplight. And her eyes dropped to gaze on the tantalizing expanse of masculine chest.

"Just this, no more," he urged, his fingers releasing the fastening and drawing the bra down her arms. Slowly Molly moved her hand and let him toss the scrap of lace and silk across the room. He took her hands and drew them away from her body while he looked at her. Then, so slowly she hardly knew she moved, he drew her to him. Breast to chest, soft to hard, warmth to heat.

"You're a pretty lady, Molly Forrester," he whispered in her ear, his hands caressing the strong muscles of her back.

"You are a gorgeous, sexy cowboy, Josh Hart," she replied, relishing the sensations that poured through her. She felt every inch of him pressed against her, could even feel the pounding of his heart beneath her breast. She tightened her arms, wanting to be even closer, wanting to be a part of him.

"Remember how you feel for your book," he said.

"I'll remember."

But not for the book, for herself. She would never forget how wonderful everything felt. How right she felt in his lap, moving her body against his, learning more of what it meant to be a woman. There was no one like Josh in the world, and she loved it.

Loved him.

For a moment, she caught her breath—stilled like a doe caught in headlights. No wonder she liked his kisses, liked having him touch her. She loved him!

And she wanted more. She wanted to learn all he had to teach her. And show him how much she loved him.

When he deepened the kiss, she responded fully. Imprinting every single nuance to the embrace, she knew she would never forget the night as long as she lived.

When he moved to kiss her shoulder, she smiled, relishing the tingling sensation his mouth made against her skin.

"I love you," she whispered, her heart so full.

He reacted as if she'd thrown cold water on him. He sat up and gripped her upper arms, pushing her away from him until he could see her clearly.

"What did you say?"

His voice was cool, his eyes narrowed.

Molly stared at him, startled at his response. "I love you," she faltered.

"Oh, no, you don't. Don't confuse sex with love," he said, his hands biting into her arms.

"I'm not. I think I've been falling in love with you since I got here."

"I don't believe this. You said you came here to work, not make a play for me."

"I'm not making a play for you," she said firmly. "I'm not making any demands on you."

"The hell you're not. It starts with words of love, then ends up demanding everything a man has. I told you there was nothing but physical attraction between us. Don't try to glorify it into some grand love that will last forever. If you can't handle it, just say so, but don't wrap it up in pretty words to assuage your conscience."

He stood up, dumping her on her feet, waiting only until she had her balance before releasing her to pace across the room.

He turned and glared at her. "I'm not buying it."

"What?" Suddenly conscious of her state of undress, Molly looked around for her shirt. She snatched it up from the floor and shrugged into it, fastening the buttons to gain a modicum of modesty.

Her heart hurt, it pounded so hard.

She felt a bit sick.

Dragging her fingers through her hair to try for some semblance of normalcy, she faced him again. He looked like the Viking warrior she'd first imagined. His hair shone gold in the lamplight. His stance, fists on hips, legs widespread and planted, reminded her even more of the warrior image.

Anger radiated from him. How could three small words have wrought such a change?

"I don't buy this bit about your love. When I got home tonight, you were flirting with Lance and every other cowboy on the ranch. Now after a few wild kisses, you say you're in love with me. Not in this lifetime, sweetheart. Maybe you like the idea of me taking care of you for the rest of your life. And finding out our kisses aren't too hard to handle, you decide to make your play."

"Stop it! It's not like that at all! You were the one suggesting we do this—for the book. This started out as nothing but a lesson from you."

"Right, but at the end of your stay, you leave, no regrets, no strings."

"I didn't plan to fall in love with you!"

"But how convenient that you did," he said sardonically.

"Stop sneering, it isn't becoming. Forget what I said.

You're right, of course. I'd be a complete idiot to fall in love with you. You don't have any love to give anyone. You'd rather wallow in the fact Jeannie turned out to be different from what you wanted her to be. You'd rather cast every other woman who comes your way in the same light."

She tossed her head, wanting to claw at the pain in her chest. It wasn't fair. She'd waited for love for so long and when she finally found it, he couldn't love her in return.

"Nice try," he commented crossing his arms over his chest.

She shrugged, reached for her discarded bra and stuffed it in her pocket.

"Think what you want, you will anyway. But I'm not hanging around."

Walking across the room proved to be one of the hardest things Molly had ever done. But she didn't falter. She'd wait for the safety and privacy of her room to fall apart. She would never give this arrogant, snide, dumb cowboy the satisfaction of knowing he had hurt her with his scathing words.

Josh watched her walk out of the room. Heard her footsteps on the stairs, the soft click of her door closing. She didn't even slam it for dramatic effect.

He couldn't move. Emotions dark and dangerous churned around inside him. How dare she try to convince him she loved him! Did she take him for a fool?

He wanted a drink.

As he left the office, he stopped, cocked his head.

What was that sound? Closing his eyes, he clenched his fists. *She was crying.* Had she confused passion with love? Had she mixed up the intimacies they'd shared with something more?

Did she really believe what she'd said, or was she just another lying schemer, like Jeannie, now distraught because her plan had gone awry?

He stormed into the kitchen, searching for the bourbon he kept in the cabinet near the refrigerator. Pouring himself a tall drink, he leaned against the counter taking another sip and another. Something wound tightly inside him as he sipped the liquor.

He never should have let her stay. He knew she wasn't right for the job, but they'd been without anyone to do the cooking for so long he'd relented. He should have sent her packing that first day. Or at least after she had made a mess of the first two meals. Or when she'd forgotten to dry his laundry. Or the first time he'd kissed her.

Mistake number two, kissing her. Or was it offering to help with her book? Had he truly thought they could enjoy themselves and then walk away unscathed?

Ten minutes ago he'd been ready to make love to her. He still wanted to. He could feel the touch of her satiny skin linger on his fingers. His lips wanted to capture hers again and kiss her all night long.

He took another drink. Glanced at the clock. Too early to go to bed. Maybe he'd drink himself silly instead.

Maybe he couldn't blame her for thinking she was falling in love. She'd confused passion and lust with something more. He'd keep their relationship strictly business from now on.

And first thing in the morning he'd call another employment agency.

The sooner Molly was gone, the sooner his life could get back to normal.

Satisfied with his plan, Josh drained the glass, rinsed it out and went back to the office to get his shirt. It had been a day he didn't want to repeat anytime soon.

Going upstairs some time later, Josh paused a moment by Molly's door, straining to hear anything. There was only silence. He wanted to knock and make sure she was all right. But hesitated. Would she misconstrue that gesture?

Probably.

He continued down the hall to his own room and closed the door, trying to close out the memory of her soft words of love.

Molly cooked a huge batch of scrambled eggs and bacon for breakfast the next morning. She had toast popping every couple of minutes and the orange juice had been poured at each place.

Furious that she'd given in to tears last night, she was extremely conscious of her swollen eyes. She wanted to have everything ready before anyone came in. She'd leave it all on the table and escape until they'd finished eating.

She'd tried washing her face with cold water, but the evidence of her crying was blatant.

With a nervous eye on the clock, she willed the eggs

to cook faster. She only had a few more minutes before Jack and Billy and the others would troop in. Before Josh would come from the hall.

He was the primary one she wanted to avoid.

She felt sick with embarrassment at her naive confession last night. How dumb did he think her? No, he didn't think she was dumb—more manipulative and money-hungry and scheming.

She stirred the bubbling eggs. Buttering another batch of toast, she slipped four more slices of bread into the toaster. Coffee brewed in the big urn. A quick glance around assured her she had everything ready. Once the eggs were done—

"Good morning." Josh's low voice came from the doorway.

"Good morning," she replied, her gaze firmly on the pan. She certainly wasn't going to run away just because he showed up.

She heard his step as he crossed to the stove and poured himself a cup of coffee. He didn't move away, but she refused to glance at him. She concentrated on the eggs, they were almost finished. She strained to hear any sound from the yard, but the men still hadn't started for the house.

"Molly, about last night—"

"Excuse me, I need that platter." She carried the heavy pan over to the platter she'd warmed. Scraping the eggs onto it, she placed it in the center of the table and risked a glance at the clock. The toaster popped up and she buttered the slices, adding them to the stack she had kept warm in the oven. Outside, she could hear the murmur of voices.

"Molly," Josh said.

She put the toast on the table, checked that everything was there, then scooted around Josh and headed for the hallway.

"Where are you going?"

"I've eaten," she lied, hurrying to escape before he could stop her.

She almost ran to her room, closing the door and leaning against it.

There, she'd done it. The first hurdle, their first meeting after last night. She hadn't handled it as calmly as she would have liked, but it was the best she could do.

The knock came suddenly and unexpected.

"Open the door, Molly."

"Go away." She pushed away and crossed to the window. What did he want from her, blood?

Josh turned the knob and pushed the door open, hesitating in the opening.

"Molly, I want to talk to you."

"There's nothing to talk about. Go eat your breakfast."

"Did you really eat?"

"I'll get something later. You better get it now, while it's hot," she said, fiddling with the curtain.

She heard his steps cross her room and tensed. She was not surprised when he put his hand on her shoulder and gently turned her around. His finger beneath her chin raised it until she looked at him.

It hurt. She loved him, had just discovered it, and he didn't believe her. He thought she thought like Jeannie, wanting him for his money.

"I'm sorry for the tears," Josh said softly.

"Josh, if you have something to say, say it, then get out. I don't need any false sympathy," she said, anger starting to build. So she made a fool of herself. Only her pride was really damaged. She didn't regret loving him, only that she had voiced her feelings.

"Last night things got out of hand. We were supposed to be doing research for your book."

She nodded. What a joke that turned out to be. Her book was the farthest thing from her mind right now.

She wished he would stop touching her. She couldn't think when he touched her.

"So maybe feelings got exaggerated," he continued.

She nodded. *Just leave.*

He sighed. "I'm not making things any better, am I?"

She shook her head.

"Come down to breakfast."

"No. I'll eat when you go out to work." She stepped back, breaking contact, able to breathe again.

Josh started to say something, thought better of it and turned to leave.

Molly followed his progress from the sound of his steps. Taking a deep breath, she turned to gaze out the window. Even now she hoped he would say something to show he wasn't totally indifferent to her.

And he hadn't.

As soon as the men left, she'd call the agency and ask Mrs. Montgomery to send a replacement as soon as she found one.

It was after nine by the time Josh finally left the house. Molly was starving. She'd been up most of the night, and only nibbled a couple pieces of bacon while she'd prepared breakfast. She went to the kitchen, stacked the dirty dishes and ran water in the sink.

Quickly she prepared herself a small omelet. But once it sat on her plate, she toyed with the food.

She wished she could turn the clock back to yesterday, do things differently.

For one thing, she would never have admitted falling in love. And knowing now what she should have known then, she would never have permitted Josh to kiss her.

How had she ever thought she would be able to walk away unscathed after such mind-boggling kisses? After the first one she should have run far and fast.

Once the kitchen was straight, she went to the office to call Mrs. Montgomery.

"Hello, dear. Are you calling about a new position?" Mrs. Montgomery asked once Molly had identified herself.

"Yes, I guess I am. Also, I wanted you to look for another housekeeper for the Rafter C."

"Mr. Hart already called that order in earlier this morning. I'm searching, but as I told you when I referred you to the place, he's not an easy man to please. I was surprised he said you could stay until a replacement could be found."

Josh had already called to have her replaced. The knowledge pierced her.

She tried to keep her voice level, all the while wanting to slam down the receiver and scream in hurt and disappointment.

He couldn't wait for her to write her book and leave, he had taken steps to find her replacement as soon as possible.

"... anything earlier, do you still wish to leave before I find a replacement for the ranch?" Mrs. Montgomery said.

"What? Yes, I want to leave if you find anything else for me."

She refused stay a day longer than she needed to.

But until something else turned up, she'd have to remain. She needed the money. And a place to stay.

"Very well, Miss Forrester, I'll call if I find anything suitable."

Molly had to be satisfied with that. She knew Mrs. Montgomery didn't think highly of her work skills. And the woman was right. But how could she show her she could do a job competently with her track record?

Turning to her computer, she sat down to work. She wasn't going to worry about doing the job at the Rafter C to Josh's exacting standards. He'd already made his decision. He didn't want her here. He could have at least let her be the one to leave.

Reading about the characters she had conceived, she soon lost sight of the problems that plagued her. She had to get them going so she could finish the book and send it off.

When the phone rang, Molly glanced up. It was time to take a break, she'd been at it all morning. Glancing at the clock, she froze. Past time to prepare lunch. She saved her work and reached for the phone.

Molly flew into the kitchen a few minutes later. It was almost time for the men to come in and she hadn't started lunch. The call from Josh's sister had taken far longer than she had expected.

She scrambled around to cut the ham and roast beef, slather mayonnaise on the bread. She heard the horses and the voices. Hurrying, she made a dozen and started over. She could fix the second round while they ate the first. In seconds she had enough to start and smiled brightly when they began filtering in.

"Missed you at breakfast," Billy said easily, scanning her up and down as he liked to do to tease.

"I ate early. I'll have more sandwiches ready in only a few minutes. Help yourselves to the tea and coffee." She turned back to the counter, began the process all over again.

Josh walked in and sat down without saying a word. He began to eat.

Ignoring him was easy with the other men present and Molly began to relax. She joked with Billy and Jack, filled up their plates again and again and made sure everyone had enough to eat. She refused to sit but kept busy running back and forth so no one commented on the fact.

"Slow down, girl, you're going to knock yourself out," Lance drawled at one point, flicking his gaze back and forth between Molly and Josh.

"I'm fine. Just a bit behind."

"Daydreaming again?" Josh asked in an obvious bad mood.

"Actually I got held up by a call from your sister. She

said to tell you she and her husband are coming for a few days and you're to be nice to Jake," Molly replied primly, refilling Lance's ice tea.

"You'll like Brianna, she's stayed here before and always pitches in," Lance said with a smile.

"She sounded nice on the phone."

Molly looked just to the left of Josh. "Which room should I prepare for them?"

"The one across from you. Brianna can help with the meals while she's here."

"I got the impression from her call that she and Jake are looking forward to riding a lot."

"Can you manage two more for meals?"

She shrugged and opened another bag of chips and handed them to Pete. "I'm sure I can manage." For as long as I stay, she wanted to add.

How she hoped Mrs. Montgomery found something for her before she found a replacement housekeeper.

She'd give anything to leave before Josh asked.

Lunch seemed to last forever. If she even glanced Josh's way, she saw his gaze on her. She tried to listen to the banter between the cowboys, wistfully remembering a time when it had all been new and exciting.

Now she wanted to leave before she made a bigger fool of herself over the suspicious owner of the ranch. She wanted to turn her back on the Rafter C and any promise she'd once imagined and find another place where she would keep to herself, do her job and find relaxation in her writing. She should have learned from Marc. Josh had merely completed the lesson.

Love and marriage and happy-ever-after were only true in books. She'd not forget that in the future.

Ten

Molly saved another chapter when Josh walked into the office late that afternoon. She glanced up guiltily and checked the time. Good grief, she should have started dinner a half hour ago. Rising in panic, she shoved in her chair and turned to leave.

"Letter for you." Josh moved behind his desk and sat down, tossing an envelope across the wide expanse.

Molly hesitated, puzzled.

"No one knows where I am," she murmured, crossing to the desk. Her old address had been crossed out and Josh's ranch address penciled in by the post office. Her heart sank, the letter was from her father.

"Thanks."

She picked it up and slid it into her back pocket. She'd have to read it, but later, after dinner.

Turning, she hurried to the kitchen. She planned a meat loaf for dinner, but there wasn't time, now, to prepare it. It would have to be hamburgers.

At least Josh wouldn't suspect she'd forgotten about the meal. She'd have everything ready when the men came in.

Dinner proved to be strained. Molly did her best to

appear carefree and unconcerned, but every instinct was trained on Josh. He ate, took no part in the general conversation, and his attitude caused puzzled glances from the men.

As soon as he finished eating, he left for the office.

One or two raised eyebrows were all that the cowboys allowed, but she knew everyone was curious about the reason for Josh's attitude.

She washed the dishes. Then, instead of heading back to the office to work on her book, she went out front and walked slowly down the long driveway. The early evening air was still balmy and the breeze that blew from the west carried a hint of the coolness from the mountains. It was pleasant and she felt a certain peace seep through her.

Now was as good a time as any to read the letter from her father. She pulled it from her back pocket, feeling the tension rise just seeing his dark, bold handwriting. What was he going to try now? Why did he feel he had the right to run his own life and hers? She slid her finger beneath the envelope flap and withdrew two pages.

He demanded she return home, forget her foolishness and settle down. He wanted to know where she was, why the phone had been disconnected. He ended saying Marc had asked after her and if she were at all smart she'd snap up such a fine man.

Rereading the letter, Molly searched for any indication that her father wanted to know how she was, where she was. To see if he had any concern for her feelings in the matter, to find a trace of curiosity for her own desires and plans for the future. Nothing of the kind. It was a demand for return, clear and simple.

She sighed and tucked the letter back into the envelope and slid it back into her pocket. Nothing had changed. Not that she had expected it to, but she always hoped that just once her father would ask about her and then listen to what she had to say. Listen and respect her own views, her own feelings, her own dreams.

By the time Molly reached the main highway, it had grown dark. She recognized the main road with a start of surprise. She had been daydreaming, again, and hadn't realized how far she'd walked. It was a mile back to the house. And it would be pitch dark before she covered half the distance. There were no streetlights, no traffic to provide some illumination. She'd be lucky to stay on the blacktop and not wander off into the barbed-wire fencing.

With a tsk of disgust, she turned and walked quickly back the way she'd come.

How could she have let herself get caught up in daydreams again? She really needed to get a better grasp of reality. Save her daydreaming for when she sat before the computer and composed her story.

In only seconds she saw headlights. Then the truck pulled up beside her and Josh looked out from the window.

"Get in, I'll take you back."

"No, thanks." She could still see the road and if she walked in the center couldn't she—

"Molly, get into the truck before I get out and put you in." His tone brooked no refusal.

She hesitated a second, long enough to assuage her pride, then conceded. She didn't want to walk all the way back in total darkness.

Once inside, Josh turned the truck around on the narrow road and roared toward the house.

"Bad news in your letter?" he asked.

Molly ignored his comment. She wanted to tell him it was none of his business. How would he feel if she parroted his words to him?

"Molly!"

"Not bad news. Just the usual stuff from my father. He wants to dictate and I refuse. I don't know why he persists." When would he get it through his head she was grown and on her own? And perfectly capable of running her own life.

Well, she qualified honestly, maybe not perfectly capable or she wouldn't be in the fix she found herself now. But it was her life and her mistakes and she didn't want anyone interfering.

"He doesn't know where you are, does he? My address was forwarded from the post office."

"I didn't tell him where I was going. Not that it is any of your business, either," she said tartly.

"Call him, Molly. Tell him you're here and give him the address and phone number. Let him know you're safe. You owe him that much."

"I don't believe you have any more right to dictate my life than my father does. Less, actually. Butt out, Josh," she said, turning in the dark cab and glaring at him. She wished he could see her.

"I'm not dictating anything. I'm only telling you to

call the man, let him know you're safe." It was a reasonable response. Why was she trying to make more of it than what it was? Was she looking for a fight? For a moment Josh was ready to offer her one.

"I'll take it under consideration," she said through gritted teeth. If that wasn't an order, she didn't know what was.

"Call him tonight."

"I believe I know how to run my own life."

"I don't think you have a clue," Josh snapped as he jerked the pickup to a stop and killed the engine.

"I certainly do. I'm managing just fine."

"From where I'm sitting, it doesn't look like it." He reached across the bench seat and latched his hands onto her upper arms, dragging her across until she practically sat in his lap. He lowered his face until he could see hers in the dim light spilling from the kitchen window.

"Molly, you can't stay here. I've already called Mrs. Montgomery and asked for a new housekeeper."

"I know. I called her myself to suggest it and she told me you'd beaten me to it. I'll be going soon."

"And just what are you going to do? You didn't make it in the office job, nor the store, nor the fast food, nor here."

Had Mrs. Montgomery shared all that with him? Wasn't there some kind of employment agency confidentiality?

"I'm doing better as a housekeeper. I'll look for another position like this one. Don't you worry about it. Maybe I didn't suit you, but I'll suit some other family, and still have time to write my book. If I can just get it published, I'll have enough money to live on until I write a second. That's what I really want to do."

He remained silent for a long moment, surprised at the fear that churned up at her declaration she'd find another housekeeper job.

He didn't want her cooking for some other man. He didn't want some other rancher teaching her how to kiss and helping her do research for her blasted book.

Yet she couldn't stay. She imagined herself in love with him. There was nothing he could do but send her away before she became a nuisance.

When he fell in love, he wanted a woman like his mother. Someone who kept the house immaculate, cooked delicious, bountiful meals, and had time to take care of any children they might have.

He didn't want some flighty, scatterbrained woman who daydreamed most of the day away, who couldn't cook beyond basics and who thought nothing of flirting with the cowhands.

Yet as she stared at him so defiantly in the faint light, his heart turned over.

She was so pretty, her eyes wide and luminous, her hair softly swirling around her shoulders, her lips tempting. He drew in a deep breath and took in her own special scent—roses.

He wanted to push her away and order her to call her father. Maybe the man could get her to go home and take care of her.

But his arms didn't work that way, they were drawing her closer. His mouth didn't voice the thoughts that he knew he should say, instead it covered hers and kissed her long and deep.

When her hands clenched against his shirt, bunching it beneath her fingers, and pulled him closer, something inside relaxed and he drew her fully into his arms. She represented sweetness and innocence, allure and desire all wrapped up into one enticing little package. And for the moment, that was all he wanted.

"Go home, Molly," he said softly, breaking off the kiss.

Her hands pushed to be released and she slid across the seat to the passenger door. Opening, she blinked in the light from the overhead bulb.

"When you have a replacement or I find another job. Until then, I work here!"

She stepped out, slammed the door and stalked to the house, the blood racing through her veins. Torn between anger and desire, she stomped up the three wooden steps and marched through the kitchen, intent on resuming her writing.

She hated Josh telling her what to do. And she didn't admire his methods one bit. Did he think he could kiss her into submission, bend her to his will through his lips? She was made of sterner stuff than that.

The emotions churning around inside right now didn't resemble love at all. She was mad enough to spit nails! How dare he think he could seduce her. She'd show him. She wasn't calling her father. And she wouldn't leave until she was good and ready.

Tomorrow, she'd send what she already had to a publisher. There was enough now for a publisher to get a good idea of what she'd done so far and where she was heading.

She closed the office door behind her hoping it would clearly indicate to Josh that she wanted to be alone.

It didn't work. By the time she had found her place on the most recent chapter, he opened the door and strode to his desk.

She heard the creak of his chair, but kept her eyes resolutely on the monitor. She wouldn't be swayed by his presence. He'd made his feelings abundantly clear. He wanted her gone. He had no use for any love from her or anyone else, as far as she could tell.

Trying to concentrate on the storyline was impossible. Excruciatingly aware of Josh, she heard the scratch of the pen across paper, the rustle as he turned pages, the squeak in his chair as he shifted position.

She knew he frowned as he read some of the reports, she'd seen him do it often enough. His soft breathing resonated in the quiet room. Longing to look at him, just once, she denied herself that pleasure. She was here to write and that she would do if it killed her!

Slowly she typed in a few words. She wasn't even sure what she was doing, but she wouldn't let him know that. She typed in more.

She'd have to read it all tomorrow to see if there was anything she could keep, or if it were total gibberish. But for now she wanted to look as if she hadn't a care in the world.

Tension filled the room, shimmered between them, grew.

Molly felt as if her nerves were stretched so taut

they might pop. She stared at the screen, trying to figure out what the words said, but every aspect of her body focused on the sounds from Josh's desk. It couldn't hurt just to glance over and see what he was doing.

Slowly she moved her head, her eyes.

He stared right back at her.

Her gaze locked with his and heat rose in her cheeks. She couldn't look away. She loved him, everything about him. From his bossy commands, to the way his skin crinkled around his eyes.

From the arrogant, stubborn jut of his jaw, to the soft way he threaded his fingers into her hair when he kissed her.

From the strength he displayed to his men, to the friendship he had offered when helping her with her book. Why couldn't he have returned a tiny bit of that affection?

Why couldn't he have let her stay to explore the attraction between them, see if love could grow on his part as it had on hers?

Josh muttered something, threw down his pen and stormed from the room.

Molly leaned back in her chair, exhausted. Sadly she pressed the keys to save the chapter and turned off her computer. She'd take a bath and go to bed. Tomorrow she'd mail off what she'd written and keep her fingers crossed.

For the next two days Molly avoided Josh. Except for meals, they rarely caught a glimpse of each other. She considered moving her computer to her bedroom, but Josh seemed to be avoiding the office, and she began to relax enough to write. She drove into town, bought some more groceries and mailed her first six chapters off.

Calling the Montgomery Agency, she told Mrs. Montgomery she wanted another housekeeping job. Apparently Josh had not told the woman the full extent of Molly's lack, and the woman promised she'd look for a similar position.

Molly hadn't called her father, but she wrote him a short note and mailed it from town. In it she explained she'd found a job working on a ranch and was doing fine. She gave no return address. She'd be at the Rafter C for such a short time, no sense worrying her father with multiple addresses. When she got her next job, she'd think about sending him her address.

Eleven

It was mid afternoon on the third day after Molly had sent in her chapters when she heard a car. She'd had so much energy that morning, she'd cleaned the house from top to bottom and done two loads of laundry. A savory stew simmered on the stove and she planned to make homemade bread for dinner. A chocolate cake waited to be frosted.

She glanced out the window, curious to see if it were Josh's sister and her husband. They were due today.

The big Jeep stopped near the back door and in only a few moments, a tall, blond woman entered the kitchen, followed by an even taller dark-haired man. Both were in jeans and shirts and looked relaxed and happy.

"Hi, you must be Molly. I'm Brianna Morgan." Josh's sister was friendly and easy to like. She shook hands with Molly and introduced her husband, Jake.

Molly greeted him, feeling his intense interest as he shook hands. He was the cop and she knew instantly he must be a good one. His entire attention focused on her for a brief time. He stood even taller than Josh and was very good-looking, in a rough, dark way.

From the way Brianna watched him, love so clearly

evident in her eyes, Molly knew his wife adored him.

Feeling a bit awkward acting as hostess in Brianna's childhood home, Molly offered them drinks.

"We want to get some riding in before dinner. Where shall we dump our stuff?" Brianna asked once they had ice tea.

"Top of the stairs, to the left."

"Good, my room as a child. Come on, Jake, I'll show you where I ran to escape Josh's bossy ways."

With a bright smile to Molly, Brianna led the way to her room, Jake following with two small bags.

So, Molly thought as she frosted the cake, she wasn't the only one to find Josh bossy. She smiled, remembering his mentioning one time he had tried to keep Jake away from Brianna. He was as bad as her father in some respects, but obviously he didn't have the ability to make Brianna do what he wanted, anymore than her father could make her.

And in all fairness, Josh listened to her on many things.

The next morning Brianna invited Molly to accompany them riding.

"Come ride with us. Josh's showing us the new dam and the pond that resulted. It'll be fun. We can make up sandwiches and eat lunch out on the range. You have to make sandwiches for the men anyway."

"I don't know, there's a lot to do around here."

"Tell her to come with us, Josh. It'll do her good to see more of the ranch," Brianna entreated her brother.

He looked at Molly, his expression carefully neutral. "Come if you wish."

She hesitated. She felt as if she'd been cooped up in the house for days. She took walks each afternoon to get out of the house, but had done nothing strenuous or exciting.

And it would be exciting to spend the day with Josh, no matter how little he wanted her. She could make memories to take out in future years—see more of his home. And always remember him as the tall, golden warrior of her fantasies.

Would she ever meet another man who would capture her heart so strongly?

"Okay. Let me get lunches for everyone, then I'll be ready," Molly capitulated.

"I'll help," Brianna said, already turning to the refrigerator.

"Come on, Jake, you can help me saddle the horses," Josh said unexpectedly.

"Josh—" Brianna began. Jake reached out and clasped the nape of her neck in one hand and drew her up to him giving her a quick kiss.

"Don't worry, Brianna. If your big brother gets rough with me, I'll arrest him and haul him off to jail." He lowered his face to kiss her again.

Molly watched with wide-eyed envy. Involuntarily her gaze moved to Josh. He stared at her, his own gaze dropping to her lips as if remembering the kisses they'd shared.

When the lunches were made, Molly hurried upstairs to get on her boots and hat. She glanced at herself in the mirror, satisfied she looked like the others. She knew she could ride well enough to keep up. And soon she'd have more memories to store up for the endless time she was gone. Josh didn't want her, he'd made that perfectly clear. Was she foolish to grasp for every little bit of time with him just because he didn't want her?

Maybe once she moved away from the Rafter C she could begin to forget him, forge a new life away from a man who refused to love her.

The ride proved exhilarating. They alternated loping across the fields and walking to rest the horses and chat. Jake stayed near Brianna, leaving Josh and Molly paired up. She kept her horse a reasonable distance away, avoiding any temptation. It was enough to be with him, to enjoy the bright sunshine, the open spaces and the grass-scented breeze.

Josh had dammed a small stream where it widened in a draw. There were several old cottonwoods near the upper end of the pond and they decided to picnic in the shade. The horses grazed nearby.

Spreading out on the blanket Brianna had brought, all four of them soon finished lunch.

Josh stretched out and covered his face with his hat.

"I'm tired," he said.

"I'm not," his sister said, springing up. Holding out her hand to Jake, she smiled at him. "Come on, we'll go exploring."

"Where?" Josh asked, not bothering to look up.

"Just around. I want to walk the perimeter of the pond. Want to come, Molly?"

She shook her head. It didn't take a genius to know when she would have been a fifth wheel. She watched the couple walk away, Jake's head already bent near

Brianna's to hear what she said.

Molly tried to imprint the scene on her mind. It would be perfect in her book and she could make sure the hero—

"We're not a pair. You could have gone with them. I meant it when I said I was tired. I want to take a nap," Josh said.

"Take it. Don't worry about me," she replied, stretching out her legs. Full from lunch, warmed by the sun, Molly felt content. She should work something like this into her book, where the heroine is so sated she felt like a satisfied cat. She could curl up in the sun, close her eyes and dream.

Molly brushed the pesky fly away from her jaw and mumbled something, turning her face away. The tickle came again. Her fingertips brushed her skin. Why wouldn't it go away? She shifted. The ground was hard, the sun still warm and the air gentle as it blew across the Texas range.

The fly came back. She brushed it away, rolled over onto her side and pulled her hat across her face. The tickle came back. Snapping open her eyes, she stared right into Josh's amused gray ones. He dangled a blade of grass against her jaw, tickling, teasing.

She reached up for it, tangling, instead, her fingers with his.

"If you sleep too long now, you won't sleep tonight," he murmured, bringing her fingertips to his lips. Hesitating a long moment, he then kissed them.

"Where are Brianna and Jake?"

If she said nothing about his lips against her fingers,

maybe he'd continue kissing her.

"Still on their walk. I suspect they stopped off for a while."

She lay still, her heart beating slowly as she let her mind imagine the newlyweds stopping for some kissing. She smiled, envious of their happiness.

And Josh leaned over and kissed her.

Shifting onto her back, Molly reached up to pull him down on top of her, his chest almost crushing her beneath his weight. His hands threaded in her hair and caressed her scalp. Even though she hadn't been sleeping well at night, she'd gladly forgo a nap this afternoon for kisses like this.

Far too soon for Molly, Josh sat up and pulled her to a sitting position.

"They are coming back," he said, rising and heading for the horses.

Molly drew her fingers through her hair, trying for some order, then slapped her hat on. She hadn't questioned the interlude, but now she began to wonder. Why had he kissed her? They hadn't spoken for days. Suddenly he acts as if he wanted her again? Or was it just that he wanted somebody since Brianna and Jake were paired?

Confused, Molly began to pack away the leftovers from the picnic and had almost cleared the blanket by the time Brianna and Jake appeared.

"Sorry we took so long," Brianna said, reaching out to help Molly fold the blanket.

"Not a problem. I took a short nap. It's nice to doze in the sun."

Brianna looked at her sharply, then at her brother as he brought two of the horses over. Jake followed with the other two. "It sure can be."

They rode over more of the range. Josh and Brianna commented on the changes Josh had made, things that remained the same year after year. Jake and Molly were along for the ride and to learn more about the ranch, but had little to contribute to the conversation.

When they reached home, Josh had one of the ranch hands unsaddle the horses. Molly cleaned up then went back downstairs to start dinner. She hoped spaghetti would suit. Brianna joined her in only a few moments and began to butter the garlic bread.

Dinner preparation was well under way when Josh came into the kitchen. He glanced at Jake in the middle of cutting up fresh vegetables for a salad, his sister helping. But it was to Molly he looked. Holding out another forwarded envelope, he glared down at her.

"This came today. I thought I told you days ago to call your father. This is the second letter you've received from him forwarded because he doesn't have a clue where you are."

"You told me," she returned calmly.

"You didn't call him?"

"No, and I'm not calling him tonight, either, so forget throwing your weight around."

"Then give me his number and I'll call him. The man's probably frantic to know where you are."

"I will not. My father has been running my life for long enough. I'm in charge now and I will contact him how and when I wish. You stay out of it."

"Call him," Josh said.

"No!"

Molly was aware Jake and Brianna had stopped working and were staring at them both. Slowly she shook her head.

"I'm serious, Molly."

"So am I. Stay out of my business."

"I'll find the number. He lives in Houston, according to the address on the letter."

She snatched the letter away and held it behind her back. "Leave it alone, Josh. It's not your business."

He glared at her.

"If you don't drop it, then I'll leave immediately," she said. She didn't flinch at his glare. She glared back at him.

In the silence the soft bubbling of the spaghetti water was loud. The hum of the refrigerator grew as she stared back. She took a deep breath.

Josh stared at her for another moment, then closed his eyes and dragged his fingers through his hair. Turning, he headed out of the room.

"Don't leave until you get another job," he said.

Molly glanced over at Brianna and Jake. Their eyes were focused on the salad preparations, but Molly knew they'd heard every word. Her own curiosity would have been in overdrive.

Shakily, she smiled. "I have a thing about being bossed around. Josh seems to bring out the worst in me," she said.

Brianna met her eyes and nodded sympathetically. "I know exactly what you're talking about. The only thing I can say is he usually means it for the best."

Molly nodded. "Maybe. But whose best, mine or his?"

She folded the envelope and stuffed it in her back pocket. Another letter from her father, and another confrontation with Josh. Maybe she should call Mrs. Montgomery in the morning and see if she had found anything promising. She didn't know how much longer she could stay on the Rafter C.

Molly headed for the office after doing the dishes. She hadn't seen Josh or the Morgans since dinner ended. She hoped they were watching television or had gone for a walk. But as she approached the office door, she heard them. Sighing with the lost opportunity to work on her book, she almost turned away when she heard her name.

"Molly's not your sister. It was bad enough when you tried to boss me around all the time. She's an employee."

"Get off my back, Brianna." Josh's voice was hard.

"Or maybe she's more than an employee," Brianna suggested.

"No."

"You watch her all the time. I don't remember you watching Rachel."

"I don't watch her all the time. Sometimes I look at her but, you can see it, she's pretty, easy on the eyes. The men look at her, too."

"There's more to it than that. I know you two were kissing at the picnic. Her lips were rosy when we got back."

"Jake, take your wife out and distract her," Josh said.

Molly heard Jake's low chuckle. "Come on, Brianna. You've said enough."

"No, not yet. Josh, you're going to drive her away with this kind of attitude."

"She's leaving soon anyway." There was no emotion in his tone.

"Why? She's great for the place. She cooks good food, keeps the house clean. And as you say, she's easy on the eye. Why get rid of her?"

"She's nothing like Mom, for one thing."

"What does that have to do with anything?" Brianna's voice was clearly perplexed.

"If you're trying to play matchmaker, you should know I don't think she'd fit in. She's much more like Jeannie than Mom."

"She's nothing like Jeannie. And if you think so, you better take a course in interpersonal skills."

"Spoken like a true college professor."

"Ease up on her, Josh. You're her employer, not her keeper."

Molly knew she should leave. It was wrong to eavesdrop. Yet she couldn't move, fascinated by the trend of the conversation. She crept closer until she could see into the room. The hall was dark, maybe no one would notice her standing there.

Jake leaned back in his chair, half turned from her as he watched his wife. Brianna sat on the edge of the desk, leaning over toward her brother. Suddenly Josh stood up and walked to the window, his back to the others.

"I know I'm not her keeper. I just think she should let her father know where she is."

"You were practically browbeating her about it."

"I know."

"You can't control her actions, " Brianna said gently.

"I want to."

"You always want to be in control."

He hesitated a long time, then turned back to his sister. "If I can be in control, maybe bad things won't happen."

Molly stared at him. The silence in the office stretched out for several long moments as Brianna and Jake also stared at Josh.

"You mean, like your mother and father dying in an automobile accident?" Jake asked at last, understanding coming to him before the others.

Josh nodded, his eyes on his sister. "That's why I told Jake to stay away from you a couple of years ago. I didn't want you hurt. I wanted to control things so you would always be around and never get hurt."

"Oh, Josh." Brianna hopped off the desk and went to her brother, hugging him. "You aren't God. You can't determine if accidents will happen or not. You can't determine who gets hurt and who doesn't. You can't change fate."

Molly slipped away, walking softly so no one would hear her. She tiptoed up the stairs and entered her room, closing the door silently behind her.

She should not have eavesdropped. Sinking on her bed, she closed her eyes, still seeing Josh by the window, explaining why he tried so much to be in total control. He was still reacting to the loss of his parents when he'd been a boy. His desire for control had arisen from the belief if he controlled things, nothing bad would happen.

Her heart melted. And her arms longed to encircle him as Brianna's had done.

Twelve

Molly tried to recall all she knew of Josh's background. Josh's bossiness resulted from the tragic loss of his parents when he'd been a child. He hoped to avert anything like it again by controlling everything around him. Probably because nothing as devastating had happened since that accident, he thought the technique worked.

Except for Jeannie. Was he even more determined to control things after her?

For a long time she wondered if Josh would always be that way, or if now that he recognized his actions for what they were, he'd ease up a bit.

Molly thought about her father and of the way his life had changed when his wife left. Had he been trying to avert another loss by controlling everything he could, just like Josh? Had that been the reason he wanted to control every aspect of her life? To keep her safe and near him. To keep him from experiencing another loss as he had when his wife had left?

For the first time in months, Molly wanted to talk to her father. She wanted to know if what she suspected was true.

If so, they needed to discover if they could have a normal relationship. If he could accept that by the very fact she was his daughter she would always love him, maybe he could relinquish some of his need for control. Loving him didn't mean she had to live her life to his whims. Could he change?

It wasn't late. She could call tonight.

Getting up, she brushed her hair, and raised her chin. Opening her door, she descended the stairs, making a bit more noise than usual to alert those in the office to her presence. But when she reached the door, only Josh sat behind the desk. The Morgans were gone.

He looked up when she walked in, his eyes dark and shadowed. He didn't speak.

"I thought I'd call my father," she said, standing near the door.

He nodded and stood. "The phone's there. I'll leave so you'll have some privacy."

He crossed to the door before she stopped him.

"Josh?"

Turning, he looked at her.

She didn't know what to say. She wanted to tell him what she'd learned, what she guessed about her father, but that would reveal her eavesdropping and she dare not do that. Finally she shrugged and smiled tentatively.

"I'll find you when I'm done so you can get back to work."

He nodded and walked out.

With nervous fingers she dialed the familiar number. When her father answered, Molly took a deep breath. "Hi, Dad, this is Molly."

Molly slowly replaced the receiver. Glancing up at the clock on the wall, she was startled to discover how much time she and her father had spent on the phone. It had been well worth it. They made tentative steps to close the breach and rediscover the love that existed between them. He'd probably always offer his opinion on what she should do, but at least he had admitted being afraid for her, and wanting to protect her from life's harsh realities. She hoped she convinced him she had to learn some of the realities on her own. They had made a start.

And she owed it to Josh.

She smiled and stood up. She needed to find him and let him know his office was free. And thank him. He'd think his bossy orders had turned the tide, and she would have to let him think that. She dare not reveal what she'd overheard.

Josh propped his feet on the wooden railing and tilted his chair back. The night became alive with rustling leaves, distant cattle calls and the stomp of the horses in the corral. His sister and her husband had gone for a walk. Molly was calling her father. And he sat alone.

For a moment the loneliness he tried to keep at bay swept through him. He thought back to Jeannie and the life he thought they'd share. Looking back, he saw clearly that she had never promised him to stay on the ranch and help it grow. She'd always been anxious to go into town, to have people visit, to travel. She liked excitement, thrills and fun times. And she'd never done a thing around the house.

Of course, he had Rachel in those days.

Would he have discovered more quickly Jeannie's lack of staying power if she'd had to do the housework like Molly? If he had insisted they stay home and develop similar interests?

It didn't matter. She was gone. And he learned a valuable lesson. When he tried the matrimony stakes again, if he ever tried again, he'd look for a country woman, one who liked ranching and cooking and didn't have different goals.

Like writing books.

He shook his head. He couldn't deny the attraction between him and Molly. He couldn't deny he liked being with her, liked her smile, her wide-eyed wonder at every aspect of ranching. But she couldn't keep her mind on her job for an entire day.

Everything he had that had once been white now looked a peculiar color of green. He knew she'd mixed something up in the wash.

Jase had found Shannon. Brianna had found Jake. That left him without a partner in the only family he had.

"Josh?" Molly peeked out the screen door.

"Finished your call?" How had that gone? "Mend any fences?"

"Yes to both questions." She came out onto the porch and walked slowly to the column holding up the porch roof. Leaning against it, she stared out across the range.

"I'm sure your father was glad to hear from you," Josh said, watching her in the faint starlight.

"He was worried about me. Now he's not. Where did Brianna and Jake go?"

"For a walk." They had gone off, holding hands, already lost in their own world of love.

Josh shifted restlessly. Watching Molly increased the yearning for his own mate.

Not her, but someone stable and down to earth. Someone like his mother had been.

"You can use your office now. I'm through in there for tonight."

"Not writing?"

"No." She glanced over to where he sat as if she wanted to say something. But she remained silent, only turning and walking back into the house without another word.

Josh heard the screen door close and knew she'd gone. He was still alone.

The next morning Molly rose at her regular time and had breakfast well in hand when Brianna joined her.

"I was coming to help," Brianna said after greeting Molly.

"No need. I've got this part down pat. Help yourself to coffee," Molly said cheerfully.

Things looked a bit better in the daylight. She couldn't get rid of the ache in her heart about Josh, but she had to look on the bright side. Her relationship with her father promised to be better. Her manuscript was already on its way. She needed to really work on the rest of it while she waited to hear when her last day on the

Rafter C would be.

"Josh was lucky to find you. He's not been real lucky with the housekeepers he's had since Rachel left," Brianna said as she slid into an empty seat and sipped the hot coffee.

"Actually, I already have my marching orders. As soon as he finds a replacement, or I get a new job, I'm gone. I'm only hoping I last longer than the four-weeks person. Then I'll hold the record," Molly said lightly, belying the ache in her heart.

Brianna slammed down her cup and stared at Molly. "Are you saying Josh doesn't want you here?"

Molly shook her head, then nodded. "I am saying that, and no, he doesn't want me here."

It hurt to say the words, and Molly longed to change the subject.

"He's certifiably nuts. Why?"

Because I was foolish enough to fall in love with him, Molly thought. She smiled gamely and shrugged.

"I'm not the world's best housekeeper. I forget to start the meals, I burn them sometimes. I did his laundry once and forgot to dry it and the next day he didn't have anything to wear."

Molly wouldn't mention the time her green shirt had bled on all his white things. Maybe he had never noticed the light green tinge.

"I haven't heard a single complaint since I've been here," Brianna said slowly.

"Probably not. For all my faults, I still beat the men having to fend for themselves. Anyway, Josh asked the employment agency for a replacement. As soon as they find one, I'll leave."

"I'd go now," Brianna said darkly. "If he doesn't like what you are doing, let him do it himself."

Molly stared at Josh's sister. If she had any pride, she'd probably do that. But she couldn't. If she could stay for a few more days, that would offer a little longer in his presence. She just couldn't leave yet.

"Actually, I don't have anything else lined up, so this is a job until I find something."

"And if he gets a replacement first?"

"I'll have to worry about that when the time comes."

Jake wandered in just then and Molly gratefully greeted him, hoping to change the subject.

Molly served up breakfast when the cowboys came in. Placing Brianna beside her brother with Jake on her left, Molly made room for herself between Lance and Jack. She was the most comfortable with these two men and liked being some distance from Josh.

Not that she could escape his angry glare every time she spoke with Lance. When he saw her laughing at something Lance said, his eyes frosted and he didn't take them from her until she rose to replenish the coffee cups.

Brianna invited Molly to join them that morning, but Molly declined. Much as she longed to go with them. The ride yesterday had been a mistake. She needed to start building a distance between herself and Josh. Somehow she had to find the strength to walk away soon.

The day passed slowly. Molly cleaned as much as she needed, then sat down to her computer. But the words didn't come. She gazed out the window for hours, thinking about every minute of her time on the Rafter C. And every second spent with Josh.

She knew she should incorporate aspects in her book, but she wasn't capable of revealing her feelings in mere words.

Frustrated, she wondered if writing was for her. Maybe she was fooling herself that she had a chance to get a book published, more than one book published. How many people made a career in writing? Very few.

When the phone rang, Molly answered. She recognized the woman's voice instantly. Gillian.

"Josh's out right now."

"Have him give me a call, he knows the number," Gillian responded gaily.

"I'm sure he does," Molly muttered darkly as she replaced the receiver. "And he probably won't waste a second in returning your call once he gets the message."

Would he take Gillian out again? Or worse, invite her over? Molly set her jaw. If he did, she'd make other plans. There was no way she'd hang around to see him with another woman.

Josh didn't come in for lunch. Only half the ranch crew were near the house so Molly didn't have as much to do as normal. She relished the break, joking with the men that had come in, enjoying their banter.

Lance stopped before he left after lunch. "Everything okay with you?" he asked.

Molly smiled. "Sure. Why not?"

He shrugged, his eyes studying her. "I don't know. Something's different. You didn't appear to be all there at lunch."

Molly avoided his gaze. "Most of me was there. I'm trying to figure out the next scene in my book," she replied vaguely. She wouldn't admit to the disturbing thoughts of Josh and Gillian.

"Want to go into town Friday night? We can go to The Last Roundup, dance a little."

Molly considered it. She had had fun last time, met friendly neighbors. She slowly shook her head.

"Thanks, Lance. Not this week. Maybe another time?" She was not staying, no need to make friends only to say goodbye in a couple of weeks.

"Sure thing. See you later." Lance raked his fingers through his hair and set his hat on firmly. His boots rang on the wooden floor as he crossed to leave.

For a moment Molly almost called him back. She remembered how annoyed Josh had been when she and Lance had gone out the last time. Even though Josh had gone out the same night with Gillian.

Would another evening spent with Lance evoke a similar response? Or would Josh shrug his shoulders this time and ignore her? She wished she could evoke some response in him.

She didn't know what she wanted she thought as she sat again before her computer. She should be concentrating on her future instead of mooning over some cowboy who didn't want her. But it was hard to concentrate on being creative when every fiber of her being longed to be with Josh Hart. She wanted to watch him work at his desk, watch him interact with his men, watch him ride his big horse. She just plain wanted to be with him.

Laboriously she began to type.

"Where the hell is dinner?" Josh roared sometime later.

Molly spun around, staring at him in surprise. He stood in the doorway, fists on his hips, frowning at her. He looked hot, dusty and tired. His hat pulled low, his angry stance looked meaner than a sidewinder. Molly glanced at the clock.

"Ohmygracious." She sprang up and crossed the room. It was almost seven and she hadn't even started dinner.

Josh didn't budge. She stopped inches from him, feeling the anger radiating from him, pouring over her like a wave.

"I forgot," she said in a small voice.

"You forgot dinner?" His low voice held a note of incredulity.

"I... uh...guess I got caught up in the story and the time just flew by."

Molly shivered at the hard glint in his eyes. Steely with contempt, he stared down at her as if he couldn't believe his eyes or ears.

"You have twenty hungry people to feed in less than ten minutes and you forgot to fix the meal?"

"I'll make something."

Her mind went blank. What could she fix in ten minutes that would satisfy everyone? She had planned to thaw some meat and forgotten. There was little choice in the pantry because it was almost time to go shopping again.

"What?" he snapped.

"I don't know, but I'll come up with something."

"Omelets again?"

"Maybe!" He goaded her and she didn't need that. She was in the wrong, but she had to go start something for dinner, not stay here and be berated. The longer they argued, the later it would be before she could get started on the meal.

Josh's hands reached out and caught her shoulders.

"I pay you to cook and clean, not sit in front of your computer all day and waste time writing when you should be taking care of this house."

"I know. I can make omelets in less than ten minutes. Make up a batch of biscuits quickly. But I need to get going."

Placing her hand on his chest in an attempt to move him, she became immediately intrigued by the slow pounding of his heart, the heat from his body, the sculptured muscles beneath her fingertips. She forgot what she was going to say. "I'm sorry." She rubbed her fingers against him unconsciously.

"You're playing with fire," he growled.

"You're hot enough," she replied daringly, meeting the silver glint of his gaze with a bold one of her own.

He frowned. "I had enough of that with Jeannie. Don't play games, Molly, I'm not up to it anymore. Go in there and fix something for dinner."

Heat washed through her. "I'm not playing games." Her hand fisted and she yanked it away from him. Trying to shake off his hands, she found herself drawn even closer, until his heat engulfed her, until all she could see was blazing silver eyes.

She didn't want a kiss. It meant nothing. Not to him, he'd made that clear. But before she could protest, before she could pull away, it changed. He beguiled and entreated until she could no more resist than she could stop breathing, Stepping even closer, she pressed herself against him and returned the kiss.

Suddenly, Josh stepped back.

"Get dinner," he said and turned to stride down the hall.

Molly swayed and reached out for the doorframe. Her knees were shaky. She drew in a deep breath and headed for the kitchen. She had less than seven minutes to get something on the table. She'd never make it.

When Molly walked into the kitchen, Brianna smiled in greeting. The place was a hive of activity. Three cowboys cut vegetables, Jake beat a large bowl of eggs, Brianna directed another man to start frying potatoes.

"We thought to have omelets, country potatoes and biscuits," Brianna said.

Déjà vu, Molly thought. Her first night the cowboys had rallied around to prepare the same meal. Had she come full circle? Would tonight be her last night here?

Feeling foolish for forgetting about dinner—and decidedly unneeded in the midst of all the activity—Molly nevertheless reached for the utensils to set the table. No one seemed to mind the work, but that wasn't the point. It was her job to do and she hadn't done it. Josh had every reason to fire her.

A subdued Molly endured dinner. She tried to join in the conversation, but, ever conscious of Josh's eyes on her, lost her train of thought more than once and was unable to contribute much. She insisted on clearing everything herself. Thanking everyone for helping, she avoided Josh. She hoped he'd refrain from making some snide comment, and felt her prayers answered when he departed immediately after eating.

Brianna and Jake were heading back for Texarkana after dinner. Molly said her goodbyes, with promises on both sides to keep in touch. Brianna gave Molly her address and phone number.

"We're looking for a bigger place, but I'll keep in touch. Come visit us in Texarkana sometime," Brianna said, giving her a hug goodbye.

Molly nodded but knew she'd never go. Once she left the Rafter C it would be too hard to keep in touch. A clean break was best.

She went to her room after the kitchen was clean. Standing by her window, she gazed out over the green fields. It was time to move on. She wasn't pulling her weight. Today had proved that. And the heartache wouldn't go away seeing Josh every day. She'd left the message from Gillian on his desk. Was he talking with her now?

Tomorrow she'd check in with the agency. If there wasn't another job available, she'd go home. Her dad wanted her to come to visit. She wanted to talk some more with him, see how far they could come in their own relationship.

She'd leave in the morning.

But when morning arrived, Molly had second thoughts. Granted she hadn't been the best housekeeper, but she had done some things right. And she would do more before leaving. Once breakfast ended, she prepared stacks of sandwiches for lunch, left them in the refrigerator and headed for town in the blue and white pickup. She'd purchase enough groceries to last them a couple of weeks. Surely Mrs. Montgomery could find a replacement in that time. And she could prepare some meals ahead of time so even if there wasn't a housekeeper right away, the cowboys would have some meals to heat up and eat.

The ranch yard was deserted when Molly returned. Quickly she unloaded and put away the groceries.

She gathered up Josh's laundry, stripping his bed, taking his towels. Everything would be cleaned before the end of the day. That'd give him enough clothes to wear until her replacement arrived.

Molly vacuumed and dusted, wiped the kitchen floor and swept the porches back and front. She had bought pizzas again. But this time she had plenty. Cooking while she continued to work, she tried frantically to get everything done. When she left she wanted the house to shine, and the men to remember her kindly.

Late afternoon, a knock came at the front door. It took Molly a few seconds to figure it out, no one ever used the front door. She hurried to answer it. A florist delivery truck sat in front of the house. A young man held a huge arrangement of flowers.

"Molly Forrester?" he asked, peering around the bouquet.

"Yes?"

"These are for you." He thrust the vase toward her.

Molly took them with a smile of delight. No one had ever sent her flowers before. Walking into the kitchen, she set the vase on the table. A small envelope peeked up from among the leaves.

"To Molly. We think you're the best! The Men of the Rafter C."

Tears filled her eyes as Molly pulled out a chair and sat down, as warmth spread through her. She blinked several times and reread the note. The cowboys had sent her flowers! She felt so special, cherished. Maybe she had done an adequate job in their eyes.

She tilted her head to the side and gazed at the pretty bouquet. Daisies, carnations, tiger lilies and baby's breath. The colors blended as tears filled her eyes. She hated to leave. She couldn't stay, but this made it even harder to leave.

Why couldn't Josh have felt the same way? Why couldn't he think she was the best?

Molly had eight pizzas on the table and opened the oven door to pull out another two from the oven when the men began trooping in that night. Smiling, she hurried over and hugged each man as he arrived.

Their laughter and awkward pats on her back warmed her as much as the bouquet had.

"Got the flowers, huh?" Billy asked, walking in last and studying the bouquet from every angle. "They look fine."

"They're wonderful!" Molly said. "I've never had anyone send me flowers before," she added just as Josh walked in.

He stared at the flowers, at her happy face, then at

the satisfied expressions on the faces of his men. Carefully schooling his own expression, he washed his hands at the sink and sat down.

"I have plenty of pizza tonight," Molly said, setting the timer. "Enough for every one of you to have your own, if you can eat that much."

"What's the occasion?" Josh asked.

Molly's eyes flew to his. She tried to smile. "I went to town to do the shopping, thought it might be nice to have pizza again," she said.

Pulling out her chair between Lance and Jack, she sat down quickly, avoiding Josh's pointed glance at the chair to his right.

"So you liked the flowers?" Lance asked after the first pangs of hunger had been satisfied.

"They're wonderful. I feel so special."

"Remember the feeling so you can write it in your book," Josh said coolly.

Billy looked up. "Are you writing everything about the ranch down in that book? Am I in your book?"

"Sure, you're the bad guy," Jack said without missing a beat.

"No, I'm not writing about the ranch. But sometimes I have trouble getting emotion into the book."

She remembered Josh's kisses, his insistence she write down what she felt. She knew he remembered as well. Why was he bringing that up now? To forge a bond between them? Ha! In her dreams.

At least the others didn't know. And wouldn't. After tonight, she'd be long gone. Time enough then to see if she could capture her emotions on paper. She'd have heartache and sadness to add to the delights and pleasure of remembered kisses. A well-rounded fount to draw from, she thought sadly.

She turned back to tease Billy about including him in her book but her heart wasn't in it and she counted the minutes until she could be alone.

Molly folded all the clean clothes, towels and bedding. She still had to make up Josh's bed. Hurrying up the stairs, she quickly put everything away and turned to make the bed just as Josh walked in.

"Oh, sorry. I thought I'd have this done already." She pulled the sheet taut.

"I heard you up here and didn't know what you were doing. I can help." He crossed to the other side of the big bed and reached for the sheet. In only moments the bed was made.

Molly had to get away. The lure of the big bed, of the sexy cowboy standing only a few feet away, tugged at her. She wanted him to cross the distance, sweep her up into his arms and kiss her like she remembered. Holding her breath for a long moment, she slowly released it. He hadn't moved.

"I put your clean clothes in your drawers or in the closets," she murmured as she edged toward the door.

"Thanks."

"I'll see you at breakfast."

"Molly—"

"Good night." She almost ran down the hall to her room.

Once safely behind the closed door, she wished she

hadn't left. It was her last night. She wished they could have spent it together—sitting on the porch or sharing a cup of coffee in the office. Wished she could have enjoyed the tentative friendship that had passed between them at one time. For a few more hours.

Shaking her head, she pulled the suitcases from beneath her bed.

Molly watched each man as he ate breakfast. She'd miss them. She'd become fond of them all, from Lance with his kindness, to Billy's flirtatious ways, to Jack's calm way of explaining things to her, to Trevor's always asking for seconds.

She refused to look at Josh. There was no need. She had all the memories of him she could handle.

When the men left, she smiled and wished them a good day, knowing she'd be gone by the time they returned to the house for dinner.

Taking her time, she prepared lunch to leave for them. Then went to get her laptop. Knowing if anyone saw her they'd immediately suspect something was wrong, she moved her car to the front of the house, out of sight of the corrals, the barn and the curious eyes of the men still on the homestead. She carried down her suitcase, and the lunch she'd made for herself. Finally everything was packed, she was ready to go.

One last walk through the old house to make sure it was in apple pie order and Molly was ready to leave.

She called the agency.

Mrs. Montgomery told her she still didn't have

another position for her, but one applicant looked promising for the position at the Rafter C.

Satisfied Josh and his men would be looked after soon, Molly climbed into her car and headed down the long blacktop driveway.

She left her father's address on Josh's desk in the letter she'd written him to tell him she was leaving—just in case any mail arrived for her. Once she reached home she'd drop the publisher a note, giving her new address so if they needed to get in touch with her they wouldn't trouble Josh.

Approaching the highway, Molly noticed the mail truck pulling away from the large mailbox by the gate. She stopped and got out. She'd just check one last time for any personal mail, then head for Houston.

The thick manila envelope gave her the first clue. It was addressed to her. Slowly she pulled it out and ripped the end off, pulling out the stack of papers.

Her manuscript. She was surprised by the publisher's extremely quick response. The letter fluttered to the ground. She picked it up, scanned it quickly, her heart in her throat.

Slow tears filled her eyes and slid down her cheeks. On top of everything else, the rejection was too much. She sank down beside her car, crying at the loss of so much at once, from her bright future as a novelist to the deep heartache from walking away from the man she loved.

Thirteen

Molly wiped her cheeks, rubbed the ache in her chest. She felt like a sad soggy mess. Beneath her the ground trembled, she felt the vibrations and wondered why. Then she caught the movement from the corner of her eye. A rider, coming hard and furiously across the open pasture. Headed straight for the fence.

Slowly she pushed herself upright and wiped her face again with the back of her hand, holding her manuscript pages and letter against her breasts.

Josh drew his sorrel gelding to a halt on the other side of the barbed-wire fence. He dismounted, his eyes on Molly. Dropping the reins, he took hold of the wooden fence post and vaulted over the five strands of barbed wire. Never taking his eyes from her, he walked across the blacktop, his spurs ringing. The hot sun blazed down on them and Molly blinked her lids to clear as much of the tears as she could before—

"What are you doing?" he asked as he drew closer. Taking in the packet of papers clenched to her chest and the tears in her eyes, he reached out for her, understanding instant.

"Aw, honey, didn't they want your book?"

His sympathy was more than she could bear. She burst into fresh tears, shook her head and stepped into his welcoming embrace.

Josh drew her up tightly, his voice murmuring soothingly into her ear. Molly leaned against him, drawing from his strength. Beneath her cheek she felt the beating of his heart. And for one last moment she felt safe, cherished.

And so lonely she thought she would die.

Taking a shaky breath, she breathed in dust and horse and tangy male scent. She wished she could bottle it to take with her. She wished she could bottle Josh to take with her. Biting her lip, she tried to stop the tears. Time enough later to give way. She had a long drive ahead of her.

"I'm all right," she said, pushing away, wiping her cheeks.

His hands cupped her face and his thumbs brushed away the trail of tears. Her eyelashes were spiky, her face had to be blotchy from crying. Great, what a wonderful last impression to leave. She sniffed, wishing she could have left before he found her.

"What did the letter say?" Josh asked gently, his eyes shaded by his hat, his mouth held tautly.

She held it out. "You can read it if you wish. It said it wasn't suitable to their list. That I need more practice before coming up to their standards."

He scanned the single sheet, then handed it back. "Maybe you could try another publishing house."

She nodded. That would give her something to do when she reached her father's. She tried a smile. "I'll be all right. It was just the disappointment on top of everything else."

Oops. Shifting uneasily, she looked beyond Josh to his horse. The animal stood relaxed in the hot sun, one hind leg resting on his toe as he patiently awaited his rider. Ground hitched, he wasn't going anywhere until Josh remounted.

She fidgeted beneath his direct gaze.

"I came for the mail," Molly said, wondering how long Josh planned to cup her face, how long she could resist throwing herself into his arms and begging for another kiss. Just one more before she left.

"That's all that came today, your manuscript?" he asked, his thumbs rubbing gently across the soft skin of her cheeks.

"Um, no I think there were a couple of other pieces." She tried to think up an excuse for not picking them up.

Josh released her and walked to the mailbox, pulling down the front and reaching inside for the letters, circulars and bills that rested inside. He withdrew the stack and glanced at each piece. Stacking them together, he walked back to Molly and held out the mail.

She stared at it like she'd never seen mail before and certainly didn't want to touch it.

"You can run it up to the house," he said.

She made no effort to take the stack. Her mind went blank and the only thing left to focus on was the steady pounding of her heart, the heated blood rushing through her veins.

Josh watched her, obviously puzzled. Then he

glanced beyond her to her car. "Molly?"

"What?" She met his gaze.

"Are you going to take the mail up to the house?"

Slowly she shook her head.

He lowered his hand. "Why not?"

"I'm not going up to the house."

With a frown, he stepped around her and walked over to her car. In two seconds he saw the computer sitting in the backseat.

"Is your computer broken?" he asked evenly, still staring into the car.

"No."

She looked out at the highway. If she hadn't stopped for one last check of mail, if she hadn't opened the envelope, if she hadn't had a fit of crying, she'd be almost to town by now and Josh would have been none the wiser until he went to the office.

"Molly, what's going on?"

"I'm leaving," she said.

She'd die if he tossed his hat in the air and shouted hallelujah.

There was only silence. A car appeared on the far horizon. Molly watched as it drew near, sped past. Slowly she turned to watch it until it disappeared. Josh hadn't said a word.

Finally, curious, she turned around to look at him.

He stared at her, his expression blank. Molly took a deep breath and with a calmness that belied the roiling emotions that churned deep inside, she walked to her car. He stood by the door. He would have to move before she could get in.

"Why?" Josh asked.

"Surely that's obvious. I can't stay, you've already asked for a replacement. I talked to Mrs. Montgomery this morning, she's found someone. I bought plenty of food yesterday, so meals won't be a problem until the new housekeeper arrives. And all your clothes are clean, and the house—"

"You've been planning this for a while," he said.

She expected more of a reaction from him. She nodded. She couldn't bear to be so near him, loving him so much, and knowing she had to leave. Couldn't he just mount up and ride away?

"Where are you going, did you get a new job?"

"Not yet. I'm going back to my father's. We mended some fences, as I told you, and I think we might be able to get along now. At least, I'm willing to give it a try for a couple of weeks."

For that she would always owe Josh. Yet she could never tell him why. "Anyway, I'm sure your next housekeeper will be perfect. She'll probably always have plenty of food, have the meals ready on time and never forget to dry your clothes."

"Probably won't dye them green, either," he murmured.

Heat flushed through her cheeks. "Oh, I hoped you hadn't notice."

He gave a halfhearted grin. "How could I not notice green underwear?"

"It was a light green."

"But definitely green."

"I'm sorry. I—"

"You were probably daydreaming and put something green in with the whites," he guessed.

She nodded. "Maybe your next housekeeper can bleach them out."

The silence stretched out. Molly felt as if she was dying by inches. Finally she pasted a bright smile on her face and gestured toward her door.

"I've got to go, Josh. It's a long drive to Houston and I want to get there before dark."

"Sure."

He opened the door for her, watched as she settled in, put the manuscript beside her on the seat. He saw the bouquet the men had sent her propped carefully on the floor in front of the passenger seat. When she was in, he closed the door.

Rolling down the window, Molly smiled again, her eyes unable to meet his. She thought her cheeks would crack. Why didn't he go back to his horse, back to his ranch and let her leave in peace?

Josh swept off his hat and leaned over until he could see through the open window. "Drive safely, Molly," he said. Then he leaned in and kissed her. A short, sweet kiss. Raising back a few inches, he studied her feature by feature, as if committing every inch of her face to memory.

"'Bye, Josh," she said through the thickness of tears that threatened to clog her throat.

He stood up, his hand still on the frame of the window, slapping his hat against his thigh.

Molly turned on the engine.

"Don't go."

She looked up. Had Josh said that or had she imagined the words?

He gazed across the range, hat still in one hand, the other gripping her car so tightly the knuckles were white.

"Did you say something?" she asked, her heart hammering behind her breasts. Surely she imagined the words.

He looked at her, his eyes curiously bright. The seconds ticked by slowly, slowly. He took a deep breath, then spoke so softly she almost didn't hear him. "Don't go."

Molly turned off the engine with shaky fingers. Josh opened the door, slid his hand beneath her arm and eased her from the car to stand before him. Dropping his hat, he drew her into his embrace, resting his cheek against her hair.

"Josh?" Molly was afraid to trust her feelings, afraid of the ray of hope that burst through her like sunshine.

"Stay with me, Molly. Don't go."

She hadn't imagined the words. Her heart warmed, filled, spilled with love for this difficult man.

"I thought you wanted me to go."

"I thought so, too, but I don't. A few minutes ago when I realized you were seriously leaving, I felt as if a mule had kicked me. Every person I ever loved left me, Molly. My mom and dad when they were killed. Jase when he went on the rodeo circuit and then settled in the western part of the state. Even Brianna, who would rather live in Texarkana than on the ranch."

"Jase and Brianna didn't leave you. They have to have their own lives. You said you all get together for holidays and Brianna and Jake were just here on a visit."

Her heart ached for the loneliness in his voice.

"And Jeannie," he continued as if she hadn't spoken. "I really loved her. She was bright and pretty. But when I found her with that cowboy, something inside died. I figured if I ever married again I'd find someone like my mother."

Molly didn't know what to say. She knew she couldn't compare to his mother. And she didn't think she could change, even for Josh.

"I'm sure there's someone like that around. What about Gillian?"

He leaned back, tilted her chin up with a finger and brushed his lips across hers. "Gillian is an old friend from high school. If I was going to fall in love with her, I sure would have done so before now."

Resting his forehead against hers, he gazed deep into her eyes.

"And I don't want a mother anymore. I want a woman who enchants me so much I can hardly concentrate on work. I want a woman who delights in the simplest things, like listening to a man talk about his day. I want a woman who can't always get the meals right, but who brings laughter and kindness to a table of rough cowboys and who is also as tough as me."

Molly's heart pounded. She could scarcely believe what she heard, but she wouldn't interrupt for the world. Josh was talking about *her*.

"Don't stop," she whispered, her hands pressing into the muscles of his shoulders as if she could pull him even closer.

He smiled, shook his head, rolling it against hers.

"I want a woman so innocent, she scares me. Yet so feminine I feel more masculine pride than a man ought. I want a woman who needs me, who—"

Molly tightened her arms around his neck. "I love you, Josh. I love you," she said, tears welling at the sweetness of his words, her heart melting at the love in his tone. Would he accept her words this time?

"I'm trying to tell you I love you, Molly," he said, and kissed her, long and hard, then easing back until it was sweet and tender.

He pulled back and gazed down into her shining eyes. With a wicked grin, Josh picked her up and twirled her around, emitting a loud cowboy yell.

Molly held on and laughed with the joy and love that coursed through her. Could she ever capture such rapture in her books?

He set her down and cocked his head. "So you'll stay?"

"I guess. Could I have a bit of clarification? Do you want me to stay—"

"I want you to marry me. We'll have a good life together, Molly. You can write your books, raise the kids. We'll hire a housekeeper to do the daily chores."

"That's wasteful. I can manage."

He hesitated, took a deep breath and smiled at her. "Sure thing. There's always omelets."

"Oh, you." She punched him playfully on the arm, then gazed up at him with all the love she had in her shining from her eyes.

"We'll have such a wonderful life together." She

paused as his words sank in. "Did you say kids?"

"Don't you want some?"

"How many?" she asked cautiously.

Josh shrugged. "As many as we get, I guess. I want someone to leave the ranch to. Brianna doesn't want it and Jase and Shannon seem settled on her place. I'd like a couple of boys, a couple of girls."

"Sounds good to me."

Four, she could deal with four.

Slowly she smiled, she could probably handle anything with Josh by her side. Slowly his mouth moved over hers and Molly rejoiced. She could deal with bossy men, as long as they loved her.

Fourteen

Samuel Forrester cleared his throat. Molly looked up and smiled at her father. He'd been visiting for almost a week. It had been a stormy few days at the beginning, but they were now closer than they'd been since she was a little girl.

"You were a million miles away," he said gruffly.

"Just thinking."

Smoothing the skirt of her wedding dress, she checked in the mirror one last time. The dress draped perfectly. The picture-book hat made her seem as innocent as Josh had said. But after today that would all change.

"Ready, honey?" her father asked. "You're sure about this?"

"Yes, Dad. I'm as sure as I've ever been about anything and as ready as can be. I thought you liked Josh."

Molly looked at her father in some surprise. He'd met Josh several weeks ago, had stayed at the ranch for a long weekend before coming up earlier in the week for the wedding today.

"I do. I just want you happy."

"I'm so happy I almost float," she said, tucking her arm in his.

"I always thought you'd get married in a church," he murmured as they walked into the hall from her bedroom. Pausing at the top of the stairs, they looked down to see the crowd in the hallway, heard the voices in the living room. For a moment Molly wondered if she should have chosen a church. The house overflowed, not all the guests would get an unobstructed view of them exchanging their vows.

"No. This is better," she said.

"Why?"

She smiled at her father. "Anytime Josh gets bossy or wants to pick a fight, I can walk right into the living room and remind him of when we exchanged vows in that very room! I figure it will be enough of a diversion to change his mood."

At first Molly had wanted to have the ceremony in their office, where they had spent so many hours practicing for her book. But the room was too small, too crowded with furniture. The ceremony would have to be in the living room. Close enough.

As the music started and she and her father slowly descended the stairs, Molly's gaze scanned the gathering. All the ranch cowboys were there, dressed up so much she almost didn't recognize them. Jack smiled warmly. Lance winked at her. Amused, she looked away quickly. Had Josh seen?

She knew Lance loved teasing Josh, and her future husband never disappointed. One day he'd figure it out, stop reacting, and the fun would go out of it for Lance.

They reached the archway from the hall and Molly saw Josh. She smiled, her heart racing. It was real, they were getting married.

He loved her as much as she loved him and today they were pledging their lives to each other.

She scarcely noticed Brianna and Jake, Jase and Shannon and their baby boy, the friends she'd made recently and the ranch hands. She had eyes only for Josh.

"Be happy, little one," her father said as he placed her hand in Josh's stronger one.

"I will, Dad, forever." Molly smiled and stepped up beside her love.

Epilogue

Molly hummed happily to herself as she drove the big blue and white pickup truck down the highway. As soon as she reached the ranch she'd go look for Josh. She knew she'd burst if she didn't tell him soon. The trip to the doctor's had only confirmed what she suspected. They were going to have a baby in a few months.

She slowed by the mailbox and drew to a halt. Scanning the horizon, she didn't see a sign of any of the cowboys. They must be on another part of the range. So much for hoping Josh would see her from the hill and ride down to greet her like he sometimes did.

The last two years had been wonderful. She occasionally forgot a meal or to dry the clothes. Josh usually said he didn't mind. And if he started fussing, she dragged him into the living room, by the mantel, and kissed him until he was in a better mood. She smiled. She liked making up with her husband.

Of course she liked it when they didn't fight. He needed no excuse to sweep her up into his arms and carry her to their bed. Or shove the papers off the desk and make love to her there. Or in the barn when the cowboys—

Molly shook her head. She was daydreaming again. She climbed out of the truck and went to get the mail. Another large brown envelope. Her heart sank. Another rejection? She ripped off the flap and withdrew the letter. Yes. This made the fourth book she tried. And this was the third rejection for this particular manuscript.

She scanned the sheet and grinned. There were many reasons for the work being returned. There always were. But like several of the previous rejections, this one complimented her on her warm and exciting love scenes.

She tucked the letter back into the envelope, gathered the rest of the mail and started the truck. Not that she had told Josh about the rejection letters. She let him offer to help her practice some more so her writing would improve. She grinned in delight. There would be more practice tonight. She could hardly wait.

Glancing at her watch, her eyes widened. Ohmygracious, it was late and she hadn't put a thing on for dinner. Not omelets again!

—The End—

I hope you enjoyed **Reckless Heart.** If so, would you be so kind as to leave a review at the vendor where you purchased it? Reviews can be long or short, they are always a help. Thank you.

Books in THE HARTS OF TEXAS Series

Rebel Heart (Book 1)

Tangled Hearts (Book 2)

Reckless Heart (Book 3)

Please visit my website: www.barbaramcmahon.com
for a complete list of all my books.